Brian Clarke writes for *The Times* on fish, fishing and the aquatic environment and has been the subject of a major BBC film for his work on trout behaviour. He is also a travel writer and specializes in wildlife and wilderness subjects. He has published several non-fiction books, most recently *Trout et cetera*, a collection of his journalism and essays. *The Stream* is his first novel. In 2000 it won the Best First Novel Award from the Authors' Club and became the first work of fiction to win the BP Natural World Book Prize, Britain's top award for environmental literature. Brian Clarke lives in Hampshire.

www.**booksattransworld**.co.uk

THE STREAM

Brian Clarke

BLACK SWAN

THE STREAM
A BLACK SWAN BOOK : 0 552 77077 9

Originally published in Great Britain by Swan Hill Press,
an imprint of Airlife Publishing Ltd

PRINTING HISTORY
Swan Hill Press edition published 2000
Black Swan edition published 2002

1 3 5 7 9 10 8 6 4 2

Copyright © Brian Clarke 2000
Map and illustration copyright © Neil Gower 2002

Set in 11/13pt Melior by
Phoenix Typesetting, Ilkley, West Yorkshire.

Black Swan Books are published by Transworld Publishers,
61–63 Uxbridge Road, London W5 5SA,
a division of The Random House Group Ltd,
in Australia by Random House Australia (Pty) Ltd,
20 Alfred Street, Milsons Point, Sydney, NSW 2061, Australia,
in New Zealand by Random House New Zealand Ltd,
18 Poland Road, Glenfield, Auckland 10, New Zealand
and in South Africa by Random House (Pty) Ltd,
Endulini, 5a Jubilee Road, Parktown 2193, South Africa.

Printed and bound in Great Britain by
Clays Ltd, St Ives, plc.

For my grandchildren

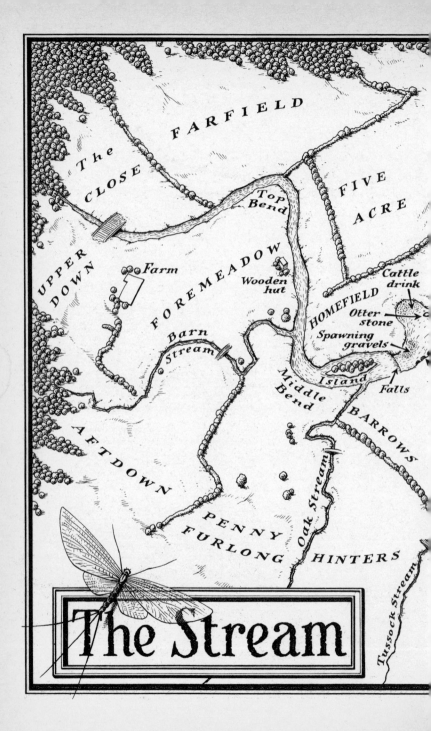

FARFIELD

The Close

CLOSE

FIVE ACRE

Top Bend

UPPER DOWN

Farm

FOREMEADOW

Wooden hut

Cattle drink

HOMEFIELD

Otter stone

Spawning gravels

Barn Stream

Island

Falls

Middle Bend

BARROWS

AFTDOWN

Oak Stream

PENNY FURLONG

HINTERS

Tussock Stream

The Stream

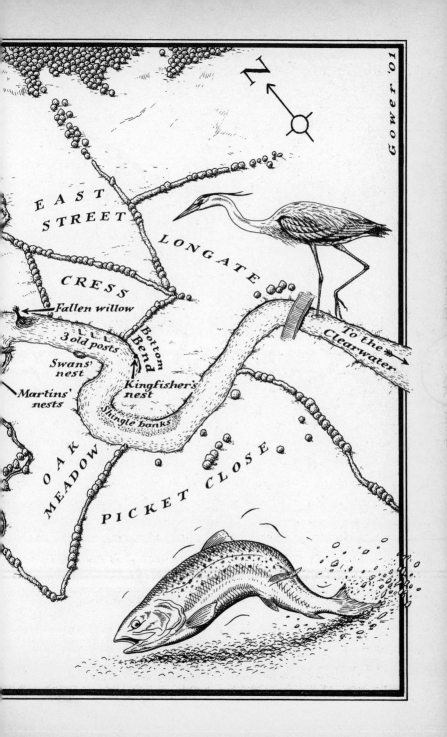

N

EAST STREET

LONGATE

CRESS

Fallen willow

3 old posts

Bottom Bend

Swans' nest

Martins' nests

Kingfisher's nest

Shingle banks

To the Clearwater

OAK MEADOW

PICKET CLOSE

Before Year One

The law of continuing, the law that governed all things, had long since made the plan.

The stream would be fed by springs that ran from the wooded slopes facing in all around. It would rise and fall as the springs rose and fell. It would rise in winter when the springs flowed strongest and it would fall in summer when the springs shrank back.

The law of continuing, the law that decreed all things, had made all life in the stream to fit in with this plan. It had told the fish to mate after the rains had begun because their eggs would need plenty of cool water. It had told the insects they should mostly come out in summer because they would need warmth and light. It had told the plants that needed fast water to root where the fast water flowed and the plants that needed slow water to live in the sheltered places.

The law of continuing, the law that governed all life, had decreed that there should only be so much water to support so many plants, so many plants to support so many insects, so many insects to support so many fish.

It had told the trout that lived in the stream and the salmon that came and went that there were only so many places for fish to live, and these were places that had food in them and somewhere for a fish to hide. It had whispered to the tiny fish while they were still curled up in their eggs and blind that the best of these places would go to the strongest fish and that if any fish wanted to own a best place it would have to fight to win and hold it.

The stream in the valley that the steep, wooded slopes guarded like a secret, ran into a big river that flowed into a great river that emptied into the sea far away. Its banks were fringed with branched burr-reed and brooklime, meadowsweet and hemp agrimony, purple loosestrife and flag iris and cress. On the banks around the island and along the gentle reach downstream from the Cattle Drink and the Otter Stone, willows and alders grew. Many birds nested along the banks of the stream and in the rushes and shrubs which bordered them and in the hawthorns that bordered the fields and in the great trees that stood in the fields. Many wild flowers grew there also and in summer the insects gauzed and hummed, catching the light.

The law of continuing had planned things this way. They had been planned this way since before the counting of the years had begun. They had been planned this way before the wolves had prowled there or the bears had roared there or the wild pigs had truffled in the loose-littered ground.

Year 1, January

The two fish knew what the plan was because the law of continuing had written it deep inside them.

They were to find their way separately to the shallows, just downstream from the falls and there the male fish would see the female and claim her. When she had been claimed and while the cock fish kept all other males at bay, the hen fish would surrender herself utterly.

The law of continuing would take her and use her. It would thrash her down on the gravels so that her tail and flank would dislodge the stones. When she had been thrashed down long enough and hard enough, a scoop would be made in the stream bed. When the scoop was the right size and depth, she would be settled into it and the male fish would be laid alongside her, his flank close to her flank.

They would touch.

When their flanks touched it was to be like a current of shocks flooding through them. A high note would come and it would fill their heads and a bright light would fine and fine to a piercing point until their whole world seized and shuddered and then her eggs would stream out and his milt would stream over them.

Once he had fertilized the eggs, the male fish would be free to go. The hen fish would have to stay a little longer. She would be taken a little upstream of the scoop she had made and thrashed down again. The law of continuing would make the turbulence she created catch under the stones and gravels again and carry them lightly downstream to settle over the eggs. Only when the eggs were covered by stones and properly protected would the hen fish be free to leave. That was the plan. They both had it in them.

And so, the moment the soft stroking of the male fish's flank left her side and the last of her eggs and his milt had gone, the hen trout moved a little upstream of the scoop she had dug in the gravels, rolled onto her side and began to beat down again. Water bloomed beneath her scratched flank and torn tail, small stones rocked and hesitated and then lifted. The current slipped beneath them and caught and buoyed them, carrying them downstream as though weightless, as if objects in space.

The hen trout gathered herself again, moved forward again over the same place in the gravels and again beat down. The currents reached under the stones exactly as written and settled them over the eggs.

The law of continuing used the hen fish for a long

time, sometimes making her movements so violent that they were visible from above. Twice the kingfisher saw her tail break the surface, its soft filaments winking in the low winter light.

When the eggs that she had laid were protected by the gravel she had steadily built over them, when they were safe and hidden under the cool, clear water that the law of continuing had always provided, the hen fish that had travelled upstream from the shingle banks to spawn lay still for a few moments until she was told she could go; then she allowed the current to carry her gently downstream tail-first, angling her fins and her body so that she was carried diagonally towards the side, instinctively seeking quiet water, out of the flow.

A little way downstream, not far from the Cattle Drink, she came to the log that lay on the stream bed and settled behind it. Her skin was dull and her belly was scraped. The red and black rosettes that had dappled her sides were scratched and smudged. Her gut was slack. Her vent was stretched and its rim was raw. She was numb and blunt edged. Her eyes were unseeing. She did not notice the heron.

Wherever the heron was, he always seemed to be a part of that place. Even high in the beech tree on the wooded slope he seemed a part of the tree and a part of the sky. His long, thin legs and broad, straight bill looked like the branches all around. His hunched, grey shoulders and white breast dissolved into the sky behind. On the ground, wary and stalking, his movements were so coiled and slow that they seemed to have no beginning and no end.

He began his glide a long way from the stream,

bending his wings around a curve of air, sliding down it until he neared the water. When he was close to the Cattle Drink and just a little above the surface, he brought his legs forward and then vertical, and then dropped.

For a long time the heron stood without moving, his long neck held rigid and high, his bright eyes moving sharply from place to place, his head tilting this way and that, straining for a movement or a sound. Then he began to move upstream. He moved with his slow, stilted, pushing gait, the only turbulence the thin, downstream trickling from each reedy leg.

A little way from the log, on the edge of the calm water that the log sheltered behind it, he saw what he often saw and knew what it meant. The law of continuing had told the heron that at this time of year, at this time of day, there was usually food to be found there. The trout was lying just upstream of the stone where the spawned fish always rested. It kept resolving and dissolving through the winks of light and reflections of clouds. Its tail shrugged slowly. Its gills pumped quickly. Its mouth opened and closed, gleaming white.

The heron stiffened, dropped his head forward and froze. The bright, yellow eyes and hard black pupils burned. And then, as though it were another part of him, in some way independent and detached, his right leg lifted a little and eased forward. His body did not move, his head and neck did not move, but his right leg moved forward. Then his left leg lifted, bent slightly at the knee and it also pushed forward, the thin vein of turbulence wriggling behind it scarcely there at all, making no noise. And then again a leg slowly and then again a leg, until the heron stood directly above and behind the trout, which had not moved. The long feathers behind his head whisped gently on the breeze, accentuating his stillness. Only the soft easings and crinklings of the stream and the low-pitched, nervous creak of the moorhen broke the silence.

And so the trout did not notice the heron. She did not notice as gradually some of the light above her went, or see the grey shade that gradually drifted into the periphery of her vision like a small cloud, or see it gradually resolve and take on firmer lines that became elongated and drew near.

It was only at the last moment that there was a long instant's dawning, a brief consciousness of something, something, and the trout brought her dulled eyes into focus and saw the heron's beak and the water surface open.

The lower bill took her through the flank, the upper bill closed over her back and the trout felt the crushing weight of air.

The heron carried the trout to the bank, splashing water and light onto the dry shingle there. Then he dropped her, picked her up across the gills and flipped back his head. The trout's body straightened to a brief vertical, the heron opened his bill wide and the fish slid head-first down. The heron kept his head high and squeezed and contracted and squeezed and contracted, forcing the fish down the way a snake swallows a frog. Then the sliding bulge was gone. The heron preened himself, uttered a soft cry and laboured on dark wings over the alders.

On the gravels where the hen fish had spawned as the

law of continuing required, the cool water was burbling and pushing through the stones. In one of the eggs, one of the eggs that had not missed the scoop or been eaten in the meantime by a loach or a minnow or by another trout or by a bullhead, or that the moorhen had not taken when she was in that place; in the egg that was safe in the space that had the grey stones all around it and the brown stone as a roof, the slow swelling and inward folding of the cells began.

Year 1, February

'OK. Tell me.' Jo Hamilton, Chair of SAVE, the local environmental pressure group, was already late. She cradled the telephone between her cheek and her shoulder, put her foot on the chair beside the wall and began to scribble on the pad on her knee. Terry was well connected. He was also usually calm. It was clear he was agitated.

'The Stinston plan is back on the agenda. For real, this time. Huge. The Minister is making an announcement next month.'

Hamilton shook her head again, slowly. 'So the grapevine was right, all along?'

'Pretty well.' Terry Summers paused. 'But not on the scale of it. This is no foot-in-the-door scheme. They're going for the whole hog.'

'What details have you got?'

'They want to widen the road along the valley from Farley all the way. It looks like Transport and Industry's old long-term plan, enlarged. They want to link the port and the south road with the M439. Instead of turning Stinston into an overflow for Farley they want to make it into some kind of hub in its own right, to rejuvenate the whole region. They want some kind of park there, an industrial park or a science park, something like that.'

'Ye gods. How much detail have you got?'

Summers glanced down at his notes. 'According to my contact, the plan for the new road will mean the old bridge at Stinston going and a new one being built to cope with the traffic. Apparently—'

Hamilton cut in again. 'What about the Frontage? What about the Hangers?'

'Let me get there, Jo, let me get there. I was going to say. The plan is to cut into Stinston Hill so they can bypass the village. The lower part of the Frontage will go. So will a chunk of the Hangers.'

Hamilton pulled the chair away from the wall and sat down, the telephone now clamped to one ear, a hand clamped over the other to shut out her husband's voice. She winced when he pointed at his watch, showing her the time. 'How sure are we about all this, Terry? We're very late onto it.'

'Dead sure. There's no doubt. There's going to be a public inquiry starting in May. They're determined to get it through.' Summers paused. 'It's going to be hard to argue against jobs around here. They're talking about attracting lots of big companies. Hundreds of jobs, thousands. In fact we can't argue against them. We shouldn't. It's impossible.'

There was a long silence. He could hear her thinking. She could hear him waiting for a reaction. She spoke at last.

'You're right, of course. This place is on its last legs after the recession. More jobs would be a godsend. We can't oppose the plan in principle.' She paused. He could hear her voice tighten. 'But there has to be a sense of balance. We have to do what we can. We have to alleviate the impact, somehow. We can't just let a beautiful valley be ruined. We can't just let a 4,000-year-old settlement and one of the last pieces of ancient woodland in the country be bulldozed.'

Summers was nodding to himself. 'I know. We're between the Devil and the deep blue. Whatever we do, we could end up looking like a bunch of tree-huggers.'

There was another pause. Hamilton raised a finger, acknowledging her husband again. 'Terry, I have to go. But we've got to get onto this pronto. You ring your lot, I'll ring my lot. Let's try to meet here on Tuesday.'

Year 1, March

The egg deep in the gravels might have been lying in a womb. The space that had the grey stones all around it and the brown stone as a roof was safe and dark. The little fish lay curled like a foetus in the soft membrane surrounding it. The noise of the current overhead could have been the roarings and sluicings within some mother's belly. The slow, rhythmic boom of the brown stone rocking might have been the distant, measured beat of some mother's heart. The threads of water that pushed and wriggled their way through the spaces between the grey stones and the brown stones on their way downstream to the young salmon that was being made ready for the sea and the nymph of the mayfly being made ready to hatch, bathed the egg with oxygen and kept it cool.

All the changes that the law of continuing had required of the egg, had been completed. Veins had reached around the membrane like a blood-red web. The flutter and then the rhythm of a pulse had begun. Eyes had formed huge and dark, big as soft boulders. An arched spine had taken shape. So had a rib-cage protecting the faint shapes of organs. Sinews had gelled. Fluids had surged backwards and forwards through conduits and junctions. Fins had splayed and stretched. A mouth had opened many times, mutely.

By the time the frosts had gone and the air had warmed and the first of the sweet violets on Longate had opened, a light had dawned in the egg that lay in the gravels, downstream from the falls.

By the time the kingcups at Middle Bend had begun to open the young trout was sensing the membrane around him. Its snugness had become a tension, its tension a tightness, its tightness a confinement that pressured and caged him. Around the time the kingcups at Top Bend were opening like hidden suns and the swans opposite the three old posts were rebuilding their nest, the young trout that felt trapped and pinioned began to push and turn. He stretched and twisted. The membrane clamped around him began to weaken.

By the time the young salmon just downstream was almost ready for the sea and the mayfly nymph was moulting another skin in her burrow deep in the stream bed, it seemed as though the trout in the egg could bear containment no longer.

On the day that the old man in the farm was being lectured by his son again and Jo Hamilton and SAVE's committee were agreeing their action plan, the trout in

21

the egg arched his back and pressed with his tail in a desperate effort. He pressed and strained and pressed and strained as though the membrane were tightening to suffocate or drown him. And then the law of continuing passed over him and touched him. The young trout gathered himself into himself and strained until his whole world shuddered and his heart pounded and his dark eyes were prickled with light from the inside. The egg's casing split and the water rummaged it away and the young trout opened his mouth as though giving a sudden cry. The stream rushed into his mouth for the first time and poured out over his gills for the first time and he drew the first breath of his new life from the water.

Year 1, April

The young salmon owned all of the stream near the Cattle Drink from the place where the sheep's tooth had lain so long, to as far out towards the middle as the flint. He also owned all of the water from there, upstream to the edge of the water crowfoot plant that one of the big trout guarded. The space was a great space. It was about as large as the shadow of a wading cow.

By the time the young trout that had hatched in the gravels was starting to make his way downstream, the changes the law of continuing had made inside the young salmon were complete. The law of continuing had long since written what the young salmon must do. The young salmon had been instructed to spend a year in the stream if he could survive it and then a year in the sea if he could survive that. If he could survive the

23

year in the sea he would grow immense because of all the smaller fish to be eaten there and then he would return to the stream as a great fish and spawn. This was the way the law of continuing had planned things for the strongest salmon in the stream. Things had been planned this way long before the man in the deer pelt had given the perfectly round stone to the girl whose smile was like the sun coming out. They had been planned this way since before the counting of the years had begun. They had been planned this way before the wolves had prowled there or the bears had roared there or the wild pigs had truffled in the loose-littered ground.

The young salmon that owned a space as large as a cow's shadow had the whole plan deep inside him. He had driven away many other small salmon and had taken their spaces because his need was greater than their need and he had eaten his fill of all that each space provided. He had taken mayflies with wings like chapel windows from the surface and Baetis flies that looked like mayflies except they were tiny and caddis flies that carried their brown wings low over their backs. He had taken the great mayfly nymphs on their way up to the surface to hatch and the little nymphs of the Baetis flies that lived in water crowfoot and the grubs of the caddis flies that built stone cases around themselves from fragments of gravel. He had eaten the grubs that reached and looped like caterpillars and that paid out safety-lines behind themselves and the shrimps that had misjudged the power of the currents and been swept away. He had gorged on the trout eggs that rolled and tumbled like weighted bubbles along the stream bed in winter. He was almost as long as the heron's beak was long. His tail and fins had darkened, the spots and smudges on his sides had faded. The young salmon was silver and sleek and ready for the sea.

About the time Tony Chadwick got back from Hollywood and heard about the development, the young salmon began to back downstream. The trout that owned the Otter Stone saw the salmon coming and watched him. She saw the fish keep to the edge of the space she owned because he had seen her, saw him drift alongside the roots of the water crowfoot plant that grew towards the centre of the stream and then saw him whirl suddenly away. All of this time the trout took no action because she could see that the young salmon was only a young salmon and was just passing through.

The young salmon travelled for a long time before resting. He passed the mouth of the Tussock Stream where the otter was hunting. He escaped by a fin's breadth when the pike near the willow made a late lunge. He did not see the heron that stood coiled as a springwire near the shingle banks but that could not reach him because he was too far away.

All through the time Tony Chadwick was getting more and more angry about the implications of the development for the house he had just built in the Broadchalk Valley and SAVE was finalizing its publicity plan, the young salmon was edging downstream, threading his way around large fish wherever he could, pausing to feed in the places held by the smaller fish when the opportunity came.

By the time the Department of Transport and Industry had given the Inspector his final briefing on the details of the inquiry, the young salmon had reached the low, planked bridge on Longate.

By the time Tony Chadwick had insisted on giving his services for nothing and SAVE was expressing its delight at having such a famous film director on its side, the young salmon had swum past the rushes beyond the low bridge and was resting near the sycamore where the stream met the river.

On the day Tony Chadwick started shooting the publicity video that would show just what the development would do to the nation's countryside and heritage and as it happened his new house, the young salmon tasted a new taste and smelled a new smell and picked up the ocean's call.

The young salmon felt the soft braids that held him beginning to loosen and fall away while the chairs in the village hall at Stinston were being set out for the inquiry. It was as Tony Chadwick's aircraft was roaring down the runway to start the flight back to Hollywood that the young salmon turned his tail to the stream and entered the river. It was as the aircraft was lifting its nose towards the wide blue yonder that the young salmon turned his head towards the sea.

Year 1, May

The old man sat for a long time after his son had left the room. He stared into the middle distance, focusing on nothing. The longcase clock ticked and tocked, measuring out the silence. It was not until the sound of the car had faded and his son was on his way back to college that the old man hauled himself to his feet and pulled on his jacket and went out.

The old man did not see the moss that covered the loose tiles or the paint that was peeling from the kitchen door. The hinge on the yard gate had been broken so long he scarcely noticed the creak It made. It was only when he had cleared the top of Foremeadow and reached the old, planked bridge that he stopped and looked around and took notice.

After all these years – all these generations, because the place was in his bones – the valley was still his escape. He loved it. He needed it. The peace of the place seemed to pass through him like ether.

What a difference a generation made. His son had always been that way, even as a boy. For all the hours they had spent together, for all the times he had taken the boy on walks and shown him the secrets, his son had shown no interest in the beauty of the woods or the old meadows or the stream or the ditches full of kingcups and flag iris. He had never once gone on his own to look at the salmon, though they were the biggest secret of all. He had never once sat by the water and watched the great mayflies hatching and filling the sky. He wasn't even interested in the family. Six generations, eight if you counted the Fletcher years, but what his son kept suggesting would sweep the lot away. Some day it would happen, he supposed, but over his dead body.

Even as the old man walked and thought, the first mayfly nymphs were swimming from their burrows in the stream bed to the surface to hatch. Before the old man had reached the gate leading back into the yard the little trout that had hatched from the gravels had arrived in the Cattle Drink. The old man could not have closed the door behind him before the publicity video Tony Chadwick had made for SAVE was being run on local television, partly because the inquiry had just opened but mostly because it was Chadwick who had made it.

The old man could not have been in his chair and

worrying about his son again for more than a few minutes before the President of Cogent Electronics was picking up the telephone in Massachusetts and hearing for the first time of the crisis in Milan.

Year 1, June

A little grew in the stream every summer. It always began secretly in the slowest, shallow water where a little had clung on through the previous winter; always the tiny, cylindrical cells growing end to end so that eventually they formed strands long enough for the naked eye to see; by summer lengthening and dividing until each single strand looked like a long, frayed thread and many strands together looked like clumps of green hair.

When Simon Goode, the biologist, was telling the inquiry about the possible dangers to the Broadchalk River and even the Clearwater if the development went ahead, he mentioned 'algae'. When the Inspector stopped him and asked if that was the kind of thing most people knew of as 'blanket weed', Goode said yes, that kind of thing, though some people called it chokeweed because when it grew over anything it seemed to choke it and kill it.

A little chokeweed always grew in the sheltered water behind the island. Most years there was a little on the insides of the three bends where the water was shallow as well as slow. There was some every year in each of the three small streams and in the long, open stretch beside Longate where there were fewer trees to shade out the sun.

It rarely spread further. It was as though the law of continuing kept reminding the long, tubular cells that they needed warm water to thrive in and that the stream was cool. It was as though the law of continuing kept reminding the weed it needed slow water to thrive in and that the stream ran fast. It was almost as if the chokeweed knew it would need more sunlight to achieve its potential and that the law of continuing was holding cloud and sun in some pre-ordained balance to deny it.

There had been a few years when the chokeweed had thrived. The old man could remember one year when it had covered all the stream bed along Longate and from the bottom of the island to almost as far as the falls and when it had choked the Oak Stream and the Barn Stream completely. In that year it had grown so quickly that the old man had sworn he could see it growing. That was the year when the plants that liked slow water had also grown beyond remembering because the rains had not come for two winters in a row, but that had been in his youth.

On the day when the first salmon of the year nosed

into the stream on its way back from the sea, about the time the old man was looking through his bank statements again and Peter Althorpe of One Earth was trying to fix a meeting with his old friend the Minister, the strands of chokeweed that had grown almost as far downstream from the island as the piece of ancient tiling, stopped growing. It was that day which came every year when the law of continuing seemed to caution the long cells and say that thus far was far enough.

The longest thread of chokeweed was almost touching the front of the ancient tile when it was stopped. The chokeweed was stopped near the ancient tile, most years.

Year 1, July

'News, Lisa! They've trailed your Stinston piece as a Special Report!'

Roger calling from the lounge. Lisa Pearce pulled the bathrobe on, wrapped the towel around her head and went through. He was on the settee. He handed her the glass she had not quite finished before going to the shower. It was brimming again.

'Thanks. Great they trailed it. These big environmental stories are so important. They—'

'I know, I know. They show man and his own future unfolding before us. Our furred and feathered friends out there, they're the human race in a few years' time. We're just like animals ourselves, fighting for territory . . . Hey!' He ducked to avoid the cushion she had thrown at him and moved over. 'Come on.

You must be shattered. Put your feet up.'

She plonked herself beside him, turned the fan to face her full-on and tucked her legs up under the robe. 'There was nearly a riot in the editing suites today. It's crazy they've not got the air conditioning fixed yet. I've never known heat like this. OK. Here it comes.' The titles rolled and she watched intently as she always did. She was a news junkie. They both were.

The US Congress story ran first, then some ructions in Parliament, then the bank robbery in Salford, then Tara Gilbey the model getting married in California. 'And now our Environment Correspondent Lisa Pearce with a Special Report on the issues raised when past, present and future collide.'

Pearce took a slow slurp from her scotch-and-water. Some nice opening shots – 'We did those from the top of Stinston Hill, above the village.' Roger resigned himself to his own silence and her asides. She always gave a running commentary on her pieces. 'That's Stinston Bridge – it's seventeenth-century. The ancient earthworks are incredible, like great stepping stones down the side of the hill. You can almost feel the history there.' Then came her voice-over bit, then thirty seconds to-camera. 'I think I set that up well.' Finally the collage of interviews she had made her hallmark, letting the people involved tell their own story. One by one they rolled up and as each one appeared, she chipped in.

'Sir John Plumpton, owns the Hanger Hall estate.' Sir John covered the ground they'd agreed – the history of the valley, the changing farm practices that had seen machines replacing people, the drift of young people away to Farley, the rising unemployment among those who remained and the general down-at-heel air. Then '. . . the Godsend this thing could be if it gets approval. It would rejuvenate the whole region, put a spring into people's steps again'. Pearce shook her head and smiled. 'Put a spring in his step, he means. He's the biggest farmer for miles around. Got fields like prairies. Didn't mention he'll make a packet if this thing goes through and they need some of his land for housing. I hadn't realized that part of the hill was his or I'd have tackled him about it . . .'

There was a change of scene, a couple of shots of container ships and cranes. 'Michael Timms, boss of the Farley Port Authority. Brother's Arnold Timms of the BBC.' A close-up of the authority's logo, a couple of lorries being loaded, then: 'Oh, yes. Absolutely. A new road to the port is desperately needed. It will speed up freight to and from the Midlands and cut costs for everyone. What's more, of course, we'd be the port of shipment for goods going into and out of the industrial park. What is certain is that if we don't get the road we won't get the development. Some people don't seem to realize that. It's not maybe one or the other, it's both or nothing.'

Roger's voice broke in. 'Oh, by the way, Pauline rang. Wants to know—'

'Shush!'

'But you've just been talking, yourself.'

'Shush! Later. I want to hear Terry Summers. I had to chop his piece about a bit. He's a member of SAVE, the local environmental group.' Summers came up, setting out the group's proposed amendments to the plans.

'Follow the line of the old B4942 to Challerton for the first part of the new road, run a tunnel under Stinston Hill to save the Frontage and the Hangers, redistribute the housing around neighbouring villages to minimize the impact on Stinston itself.' A few other tweaks here and there. Then the crunch. 'Yes, the tunnel would cost more. Yes, millions more. But we can't just put concrete over everything.'

Then Jo Hamilton. 'Damn, Keith's cut a bit . . . Hamilton's the leader of SAVE. Tricky for her. Walking a tightrope with the environment on one side and jobs on the other.' Up came Hamilton acknowledging the region's decline and the need for jobs, Hamilton talking of the irreplaceable woodlands and the 4,000-year-old settlement and the need to protect the Broadchalk and the Clearwater and their plants and wildlife. 'The Ministry is refusing to look at the alternatives we've put forward on grounds of cost but not a penny's value has been placed in their scheme on our history and heritage and the loss for ever of this beautiful landscape.'

Pearce sucked her teeth. 'Damn again. There's another cut. Must have been to make room for the Gilbey wedding. Broke late.'

Then it was Dame Vanessa Bennett. 'You remember Dame Vanessa, married to Samuel Bennett, the conductor?'

Roger nodded. 'Isn't she the one who wrote that letter to *The Times*, really put this thing on the map?'

'Yes. She's as much a philosopher as she is a naturalist. A great old girl, eighty if she's a day. And she sure knows how to use the camera. Just look.'

Bennett's eyes were looking straight into the room,

as though she were speaking to the two of them directly. 'Well yes, of course we need progress, but whose definition of progress are you proposing we adopt? . . . What we may be about to do here can never be undone . . . Every time we do something irrevocable to meet our own needs we are limiting the options our children will have to meet theirs.'

The moment her piece was over, Pearce hit the remote control and the sound went down. 'Well, what did you think?'

'Wonderful. Brilliant. Liked the old girl. Profoundly moving et cetera et cetera. Seriously, though, a good piece. Now are we going out or aren't we?'

'What did you say Pauline wanted?'

Year 1, August

The swans always nested opposite the three old posts that stuck out of the water just upstream from Bottom Bend. The dense rushes there provided all that the swans needed for building and repairing and the bank of the small bay made it easy to walk down into the water and easy to climb out again, even for cygnets. That place also gave a good view as far downstream as the kingfisher's nest and as far upstream as the Cattle Drink.

The cob and pen owned most of the stream that was big enough for swans. They owned all the water upstream to the falls and downstream around Bottom Bend and along the shingle banks below that, almost as far as the old, low bridge on Longate. All this water swayed with the bright water crowfoot plants that swans like so much and, in summer, the surface was covered with the small white daisy-flowers the lush growths produced.

The cob had been made to fight for the stream when he first arrived. He had driven off the older bird that already owned it, the one that had damaged a wing on the fence-wire a few days before.

The old bird had been bigger but had been weakened by the deep red bite that the wire had taken from his wing when he glided in to land and the younger bird had driven him away. Then the young cob had driven him away again twice more when the old bird returned with a healed wing, each time the fight being shorter than the last because though his wing was strong again the damage of the first beating had taken root in the old bird's brain and the confidence of the first victory had given the young bird new strength.

The cob had fought off challenges from other birds every year since and he spent much time in the summer patrolling upstream and down, chasing off the migrant flocks of young males looking for places of their own. Mostly when the young birds saw the size of the cob and could see from the menace in him that he owned the water, they turned tail and lowered their necks in submission and hurried away. From time to time one of them would hold its ground because it needed a place of its own badly and then the cob would have to fight. Once, the cob had needed to kill an intruder in the way the law of continuing had told him. He had beaten the other bird with his wings harder than that bird had beaten him, and then he had twisted his neck around its neck and scrambled onto its back and forced its head under water like one man wrestling another's arm down on a table. But mostly it had not come to that.

The last of the swans' eggs had cracked and opened on the day that the mayfly nymph above Middle Bend hatched, around the time the nymph was still clinging to the rim of his burrow in the stream bed with the currents racing around him and buffeting and jostling him like a heavy wind.

Ever since that day the adults had stayed close to their young to protect them. When they left the nest together, the cob leading, the cygnets behind and the pen guarding the rear, it was so that the cygnets could get to know their water and practise the skills the law of continuing had given them. They practised controlling how fast they drifted downstream by facing upstream and paddling. They practised turning slowly on the water by hanging one foot down and letting the current push against it. They began to practise spinning quickly on the water by holding one foot down and paddling with the other.

The cygnets ate drifting nymphs and hatching flies and some of the things that were not to be eaten until they learned better. They ate well of the young shoots of water crowfoot beneath the bright white flowers that swept over the surface and that broke the sunlight into dazzling slips which flicked into their eyes. The cygnets were not frightened by much because of the way the cob and the pen protected them, but they were startled the first few times a dragonfly rattled near their heads and they had a high time lunging and scrambling after the bright blue damsel flies once they had got used to the way they darted and zipped.

On the day when the President of Cogent Electronics

bawled out his Director of Manufacturing and Development for the mess in Milan, around the time SAVE's publicity co-ordinator was dreaming up the idea of the aerial shot showing hundreds of people lined up on the Frontage and spelling out NO NO NO, the pen heard the cob give his low, harsh rasp and saw him stiffen.

By the time she had seen the stranger feeding near the mouth of the Tussock Stream and the cygnets had quickly turned and clustered about her, the cob was already gathering himself into himself and arching his neck over his back and was pushing his breast out like the prow of a galleon. It was as if the cob had felt a sudden heat flooding through him and had seen a redness behind his eyes and had felt a blackness as hard as a hammer lock the back of his brain. The cob lifted his wings and seemed to pump his anger into them until they swelled up around him and filled him with menace.

The cob looked to neither side nor behind. He drove himself down the line of his eyes, pushing down with both feet together, each forward urging making the water surge up his breast, each downward thrust causing it to well up in his wake beneath puddles of domed light.

Even as he was closing the space between them, the cob saw the intruder uncoil its neck from the water and saw the water gleaming from its head and the strand of water crowfoot dripping light from its beak. Then he saw the intruder look at him as though he were not there and reach under the surface again and pull up another strand. The movement seemed to madden the cob even

41

more. He began to half-run over the surface and half-fly, rocking and splashing with his neck stretched out like a flexing lance.

The intruder that had come because it needed that place and that had seen the cob charging, was ready. He lurched to one side to avoid the big cob's rush and turned to face him head-on.

For a long time the two birds fought, lurching and circling, circling and lunging, all the time beating one another with their wings and trying to climb onto one another's back and reaching across one another's neck with their own neck so they could wrestle it under water.

The intensity of the fight made a silence of its own except for the noise the two birds made themselves and the cheeping of the cygnets and the gossiping of the ducks that spun on their axes. The vole under the alder blinked at the commotion and the bullocks on the bank jostled to get a better view. Waves surged up the banks and slopped into the bays and a long brown slick of weed and silt and muddy feathers and dust clouded the water past Bottom Bend.

Then, abruptly, the challenge ended. The intruder turned away with his spirit suddenly broken and his strength almost gone. He swam with his neck lowered and his head turned a little to one side so that he could keep the cob in view. The cob surged after him with his neck arched back like a threatening snake and his wings curved upwards and back as if pumped full of triumph. He chased the intruder all the way past Bottom Bend and around the shingle banks to the place where his territory ended near the low bridge.

For a long time after that, while the cygnets cheeped and the pen stood high on the nest where she could see upstream and down, the cob re-ordered himself and pulled out the twisted feathers that would not go back and put the others back in place and brushed himself all over with the side of his head until he was sleek and clean.

It was evening, when the sun was sinking and the stream was flooded with a rosewater light, before the swans made their way along the margins again, the cob slowly leading with his head held high and his hard eyes watchful, the pen at the rear making low sounds that the cygnets answered.

It was evening, as the stream was flooded with a rose-water light and the swans were travelling in single-file again, when the Inspector sketched out his note about the danger to the two rivers if either were abstracted to supply water to the development. The following day he drafted his advice for the Minister.

Year 1, September

'Remember the Aces?'

There was a long silence. The Minister signed the last of the letters in the fat 'For Signature' folder and slid it to one side of his mahogany desk.

He looked around the cavernous room in a mock-studied way, theatrically moving his gaze from the great chandelier in the centre of the ceiling down and along the walls, first to the painting of the Battle of Stamford Bridge (colourful but wooden), then to the extraordinary painting by whoever-it-was of the construction of the Forth Bridge (all girders and sky and fisherfolk in smocks), then one by one along the photographs of his predecessors (including the one of Sparshot who, according to the new biography, had been a liar and a philanderer, though up there on the wall he looked like a lay preacher dressed for Sunday).

Then he smiled. 'At a guess, Peter, that is the first time the Aces have been mentioned in this room. Yes, of course I remember the Aces. It's all right for Ministers to remember their childhoods. Some Ministers actually had childhoods, you know.'

Peter Althorpe looked back at his old friend. A long way to come, leader of the Aces to Cabinet Minister, but then the lad who had once lived next door had always been the one who was going to make it big, if any of them did.

'Then you remember the cave. And you remember the sickle-shaped stone or whatever it was – the one I found in the river at Stinston Meadows?'

'Of course I remember them. We thought the stone was a fossilized bear's claw or something. We used to play Stone Age men in the cave at the Frontage.'

'Great days. Great memories. You couldn't put a price on memories like those.'

'Yes, great days.' The Minister paused and studied his friend in turn, looking straight into his eyes. 'Peter – are you trying to say something?'

'The cave will go if this thing goes through. There are going to be lots of small losses no-one's focusing on yet.'

There was a pause. 'I didn't know. That's a pity.' The Minister swivelled in his heavy chair and stood up. He walked over to the high, draped windows that looked across the Thames, shimmering in the heat. It had been the same rainless, baking view for months. Then he turned.

'Look, Peter, I've got a job to do.' He studied the man who had just been studying him. One Earth was not the biggest environmental lobby group but it was one of the most active and probably the most respected. Peter had given it real clout since he'd become Director.

'I've got a job to do,' the Minister said again. 'I'm as concerned as you are about the valley, the river, everything. Yes – and the cave. It's where my roots are, for heaven's sake. But I can't let any of that get in the way of this decision. Not in a personal way.' He waved out of the window. 'What those people out there expect' – his voice tightened – 'what the PM expects, is that I'll do everything I can to get jobs and investment into anywhere I can. I have to deal with the world as it is, not as I'd like it to be.'

Althorpe stood up and bent backwards with his hands behind his hips, easing the ache in the small of his back. Damned back. 'I know you can't. I'm not asking you to let personal feelings creep in. But you've seen our input. I'm asking you to acknowledge the real world in everything. If this thing goes through, that place is lost for ever. You know there are intangibles involved in this that are real, even if they're difficult to quantify. Every decision you've ever taken has involved some subjectivity. That's what I'm asking you to acknowledge, now.'

Althorpe moved over to his friend and they stood side-by-side, looking out. 'If we go on at this rate, you know, our kids will end up living in bunkers breathing oxygen from cans and being told what grass looked like. I'm not asking you to veto this, of course I'm not. I'm asking you to alleviate the worst effects along the lines we've proposed.' He lowered his voice. 'Save the Hangers and the Frontage. Buy our proposal for the tunnel – that's what I'm asking you to do, bottom line.'

The Minister waited to see if there was any more. Then he shook his head. 'My people have already made it clear a tunnel's out of the question, whatever the Inspector recommends. It's out of the question.' The way he repeated the phrase made the words sound as if they were spoken in italics. 'The Treasury's strapped. The Chancellor's dealing in small change. This has been the deepest recession in twenty-five years, you know that.'

He turned from the window, walked back to the desk, sat down and looked up. 'Look, Peter, we're not near a decision yet. The inquiry's still sitting, for God's sake. But I do have to tell you this. If I conclude we can get this thing off the ground successfully and to do that it has to go ahead precisely as proposed, I won't hesitate. I'll cut corners if I have to. I'll make life easy for anyone with an idea and cash to invest.' He shook his head. 'I won't be telling Mrs Bloggs that she can't have her hip done because we used the money to build a tunnel to save some old bones. I won't be telling her son he can't have a job because we decided someone else's past was more important than his future.'

Althorpe half-nodded. 'And you know I can't accept that, old lad. You know it's nothing personal but if this thing goes ahead, we're going to make life difficult down there. The Frontage and the Hangers aren't the only issues – there are the rivers, the wildlife, every-thing – but we'll focus on the woodland and the settlement because they're visible and uncomplicated and Joe Public can understand them.' He put out his hand.

The Minister smiled a wan smile as he stood up and took it. 'No, I won't take it personally, Peter.' He paused. 'If I were in your shoes I'd be doing exactly the same, sticking with the Frontage and the Hangers. If it's out of sight it's out of mind as far as the public's concerned. If it's not furry and cuddly or something out of Walt Disney, they don't want to know.' He put his arm around his old friend's shoulders as they walked to the door. 'Don't quote me on that, old lad. That was the human being speaking, not the Minister. You know Ministers aren't human, don't you?'

'Known it all along,' said Althorpe.

Year 1, October

The young trout that had been born in the gravels downstream from the falls owned a great space in the Cattle
Drink. He owned the large stone that had the grubs
of the caddis flies all over it and the stone under that
and the round stone he had used for hiding under when
he was small. He also owned several more stones
further towards the middle where the fast water began
and three more nearer the bank and a small one behind.

The young trout owned all the triangles of silt that
the water had dropped behind the stones and all the
mayfly nymphs that had tunnelled into the silt. He
owned the calm places in front of the stones where
the current was slowed and deflected. He owned all the
small currents that slid around and between and over
the stones and all the food they carried and all that lived

in the two fronds of water crowfoot including the nymphs of the dainty Baetis flies and the caterpillars of the little black flies and the grubs of the caddis flies that lived in tubes they made from fragments of gravel. The space that the young trout owned was a great space. It was about as wide as a heron's wing is wide and about as long as a heron's leg.

The trout that was more than half as long as the old man's middle finger had listened well when the law of continuing had spoken. He had driven many other fish away to claim such a space. Sometimes the other fish had made him fight but mostly he had been able to frighten them off by using the threat that the law of continuing had told him to use. When he needed a space another fish owned he soared up a little in the water and looked down at his opponent and flared his gills so that his head looked big and he opened his jaws wide so that they looked fierce and terrible. Weaker fish often gave ground in the face of this threat and much fighting was avoided.

The trout that owned the space in the Cattle Drink had shaped the stream around him so that it fitted him closely and all the powers of the currents moved through him. He could use the water the way a swift uses air. He could so angle his fins that he could soar and slip and dive without effort. He could so perfectly place himself in the path of a drifting nymph that the water would carry it right into his mouth.

The trout could spot the caddis larvae that built cases of pebbles and sand around themselves even when they were on the stream bed and looked like gravel upon gravel. He could pick off the small, low nymphs that clung to the stones in fast water and he could dislodge the nymphs of the dainty Baetis flies from the plants so that he could take them mid-current. He could slide up and intercept the nymphs that were hatching into flies at the surface before flying away. Sometimes he could even leap up and catch the brown-winged caddis flies that flew over the water at dusk, though often he missed them because the law of continuing had told him nothing of refraction. The trout that had hatched in the place that had the grey stones all around it and the brown stone on top had olive-brown on his back and gold on his flanks and white on his belly. Red spots and black spots freckled his sides. When the sun took the light and melted it over him, it was as though he dissolved in midwater.

By the time the Inspector had passed his report to the Minister and the President of Cogent Electronics had seen the remarkable technology his researchers had code-named 'Fairway', the young trout seemed to be as much a part of the stream as the water. It sometimes seemed that the young fish that angled and darted, splashed and rolled, was water itself in a firmer form.

Year 1, November

Pretty well everyone in the public gallery recognized someone else there, other than the Japanese who were flying out that evening and the two Germans and the man from Gothenburg who had always wanted to see the British Parliament because of his fascination with the way one tiny country had once ruled so much of the earth. In fact, as Peter Althorpe whispered to Jo Hamilton, it looked a bit like a lobbyists' club. It looked like a reunion of every lobby and vested interest group that had followed every major planning development over the last fifteen years.

Hamilton recognized many of the faces herself. Jim Hampton, of Hamptons, was three seats along. She'd learned that Hampton had known the detail about the development before SAVE had even been tipped off. Sir

John Plumpton was just to Hampton's right. Plumpton's family had owned the Hanger Hall estate for over 300 years. Made a fortune out of farming yet the estate was still in debt, God knew how. Gossip was that if the housing plan went through, Plumpton would make enough to wipe out the debt several times over and still be left with a packet. Keith Arthur, the County Council's Chief Planning Officer, was directly behind Plumpton. Deirdre Weston, who had represented National Heritage at the inquiry, was just behind him. She had put up a pathetic performance, scarcely said boo, yet NH was supposed to be guardian of the nation's landscape and birthright. NH were not going to rock any boats just yet, not after the Scarborough business, everyone knew that. But the way they had rolled over on this had been amazing. NH knew their card was marked. They were neutered for the time being.

Peter Althorpe nudged her and indicated several faces that were unfamiliar. Someone from the National Drivers' Association over there. Someone from the Road Haulage Confederation alongside him. Both were pushing furiously for the road, of course. Two men in dark suits, the one on the left from Plantains, the civil engineering giant, the one on the right from Greenmount, ditto. And oh, yes, Dame Vanessa Bennett in the corner at the back. She'd just had another letter in *The Times*.

The Minister smiled when he looked up from the Government Front Bench. The local media would make it sound as though the eyes and ears of the world had been hanging on his every breath, but there were more visitors in the Gallery than there were Members in the House.

Yes, he said, when he eventually leaned over the Despatch Box in that bizarrely awkward posture Ministers use to suggest ease, the development would go ahead as planned. Alternatives put forward on some points of detail would offer aesthetic and in some cases practical improvements and these would be incorporated wherever possible. There had been many representations about the site known as the Frontage and the piece of ancient woodland called the Hangers but changes to protect these completely could not be made without creating new problems and incurring unacceptable additional cost. He had, however, accepted his Inspector's recommendation that special measures be taken to protect both the Broadchalk River and the Clearwater River and their remarkable fauna and flora. Specifically, neither would be abstracted to supply water for the development and quite exceptional precautions would be taken to ensure there could be no pollution. He had been told that archaeologically important finds could be made in the course of the work around the Frontage. He would ensure that moneys from the National Historical Fund were available to house them appropriately in the museum at Farley.

'After so many years of decline – most of them, I have to say, a direct result of the policies of the party opposite – the entire region can look to the future with new hope.

'There will be new investment, new jobs, improved road communication from the port to the development complex and from the development to the motorway network.

'A wave of prosperity will roll out from the Broadchalk valley to the communities around it. This is a good day for Stinston, a good day for Farley, a good day for Britain.'

It was as he said 'a good day' for the third time that the piece of silt that had once been part of the shell of one of the snails that used to live above Top Bend, whirled over the head of the young trout in the Cattle Drink and settled behind him. It was so tiny that the little trout did not see it. No silt had settled in that place in winter, since the old man's son had been a child.

Year 1, December

It might have been because there had been no rain and the stream was so low. It might have been because there had been no rain yet and there was less water than there should have been to disguise his outline.

It might also have been because the water crowfoot had died back as it does in winter and there was less cover to hide him.

It might easily have been because the stream was so low and the water plants had died back and because he had an ache in his gut. All the fish had aches in their guts, even the ones that the law of continuing had not touched in readiness for spawning. Winter was the time when all the fish went hungry because everything they ate was in hiding or only half grown. So it might easily have been because he was easier to see and distracted by hunger that it happened.

It might even have been that the kingfisher herself was distracted and misjudged her dive, but when she dived on the fish she could see clearly and yet only glanced it, the trout that had hatched in the womb in the gravels with the grey stones all around and the brown stone on top was given a wound in his flank that burned like fire and a scar that would mark him for ever.

Year 2, January

Every year a trout spawned, it spawned in the same place. The fish upstream of the falls spawned in the shallow water above Top Bend and most of the trout downstream from the falls spawned close to the Cattle Drink. A few fish used the three tiny streams to the west.

All of these places were perfect for spawning because the law of continuing had made them that way. The stones in the gravels there were of the right size, which is to say a little larger than a big trout's eye and the water there was the right depth, which is to say about as deep as a big trout is long.

The law of continuing had taken special account of the eggs when the gravels were made. It had decreed that the currents should be so fast over the gravels that no silt could settle over them. In the exact places on the gravels where the fish had been told to dig their scoops, the law of continuing had provided springs to well up from the stream bed so that the stones and the eggs could be washed clean from below. In the interests of the fish as well as their eggs, the law of continuing had decreed that the water in the stream should always be cool because cool water could carry more oxygen than warm and the fish as well as the eggs would need a lot of oxygen to survive. There was no small thing, not even the uttermost small detail, that the law of continuing had not made perfect for the fish that needed to spawn.

It was in the week that shares in Plantains and Greenmount soared because of the contracts they had been awarded for work on the development that the hen fish opposite Longate moved. On the day the old man was worrying about his bank statements again and his son was again urging him to modernize the farm, the hen fish began to swim steadily upstream, following the route that the current had marked out. The hen fish from opposite the shingle banks followed soon after and then the hen fish and the cock fish that had held lies close together near the kingfisher's nest, moved in behind them both.

In ones and twos other fish drifted in behind them and followed, sidling through the currents and forging softly through the pools, working their way upstream like aimed shadows, gradually uniting into a threaded queue around the insides of the bends and the outsides of the gravel bars. It was only on the spawning beds that they spread out and paired.

Some fish found the places they wanted and began to dig straight away. The hen fish from Longate took time.

She lay for days over the space she had chosen, seeming to measure and test it, drifting this way and that while the cock fish that had claimed her drove all challengers away.

It was on the day when the woods beyond the valley were echoing to the high calls of men and the whirr of pheasants' wings, about the time that the first shot was piercing the crisp, thin air, that the law of continuing rolled the hen fish over.

The law of continuing gave her no mercy. It thrashed her on the gravels from first light. It thrashed her so hard that her sides became scratched and her scales became loosened and her tail became ragged and torn. Little by little a scoop was dug.

When the scoop in the gravels was the right size and the right depth, the law of continuing laid the hen fish into the space and laid the cock fish beside her. The moment his flank touched her flank the law of continuing consumed them both. She felt a great tension arise and shake her, then a light fined to a bright point inside her head and she heard a high note singing and singing until it snapped and her jaws were wrenched wide and her eggs spilled out in a rush. As her eggs were taken, the cock fish that had fought away all others for this one moment alone was given a brighter light of his own and his own high note and his milt was removed.

When the two fish were drained and spent and their high notes had gone and their bright lights were bleached and flat, they separated. The cock fish backed downstream and the hen fish covered her eggs with stones and the President of Cogent Electronics called the meeting.

When the hen fish was satisfied that her eggs were safe she drifted downstream ragged and spent, then sidled across the current towards the log where spawned fish often rested and rested there.

It was almost dark when she headed back to Longate. It was almost dark when the fox found the scales of her mate glinting on the bank and smelled the smell of the heron that had taken him. It was almost dark before the young man stopped pressuring the old man again and the old man went to his room and looked at the photographs of the farm as it had always been and felt the leaden weight inside.

Year 2, February

David Hoffmeyer had listened intently, his deep chair canted back and rocking lightly, his legs casually crossed, his elbows on the armrests and his fingertips together, saying nothing.

Ron Garnet, Chief Development Engineer for Cogent Electronics, clicked the button on the remote control. The last graph disappeared, the screen went black and the teak doors that thirty minutes before had slid noiselessly open, slid noiselessly closed. Garnet pressed the button under the table. The curtains in the window waltzed to a rhythm of low click-clicks and the New England sunlight flooded in.

Garnet slipped into the chair next to his boss, Jack Visconti. Hoffmeyer, Cogent's President, looked down the table.

'Gentlemen?'

There was a pause. It was as though everyone was waiting for a ball to stop bouncing. Hoffmeyer's easy dominance of his Executive Board often had that effect when there was a big decision to be made. No-one wanted to step in first. No-one got to be President of the third biggest electronics business in the US without being able to blow hot as well as cold. They had all been burned at one time or another.

Hoffmeyer turned. 'Jack?'

The Director of Manufacturing and Development pursed his lips and then nodded. 'Nothing to add to what Ron and his team have just told us.' Visconti nodded towards Garnet. 'The M and D perspective is clear. We need a high skill base, reliable suppliers, the right costs. We need a sophisticated infrastructure – especially good roads and access to a port as well as an airport. If we're going to put this facility into Europe – and we've already been through that – it's got to be Germany, Italy or the UK.'

'And you want Germany.' It wasn't a question.

'Fairway technology has tremendous potential. The Japanese are behind but they're working on something similar. We need the smoothest fast start we can get. We've got the lab and the plant in Germany, lots of skilled people we can pull out temporarily. We can get this programme up and running with them while we train the new staff we need.'

Hoffmeyer drank the last of his coffee. 'No problems with infrastructure. No problems with the Government. What about costs? German costs are high. And we can't have another Milan.'

Visconti grimaced. 'David, Milan is fixed. It's taken care of. Yes, I'm happy about costs.'

Tom Spicer, Global Director of Marketing, had been leaning back in his seat with his arms outstretched, palms flat on the table. He made a scarcely perceptible movement with his right index finger and drew instant attention. 'I know what Jack's saying. From an M and D perspective he has to be right – in the short term, anyway. But if you follow his logic you end up putting everything into Germany.'

Hoffmeyer gave him a nod. 'Go on.' He knew what was coming. Spicer had called him the moment the agenda had gone out.

'From a marketing perspective – from a whole-business perspective – this is a political decision as much as anything. Italy still frightens me after Milan. I agree the only real choice is Germany or the UK. But we should go for the UK. We've got a big piece of the German market already. We're late into the UK for the reasons we all know. There's massive opportunity there, huge Government business to be won. If we could get some Government business in the bag we'd have a base. Then we could go after other sectors. But if we want Government business we've got to do something to earn it. We've got to give them good reason to buy from us. There's no shortage of competition.'

Nick Brewster, Director of Corporate Affairs, cut in. Spicer had given him the cue they'd agreed. 'What Tom's saying makes sense. Yamahatsu have a plant in Scotland, Gong have pretty well everything UK-based through their ownership of Britcom. They get

Government business because they invest in the country. If we can show the Government we're just as committed to the UK as the Japs are, put down some roots there, create jobs, they'll have an incentive to deal with us. I think the idea of getting Fairway technology into the UK early would bowl them over. There'd be so many spin-offs. After the recession they've been through, I think they'd bite our hand off. They'd push business at us to get us in and keep us in.'

It was a long time before Hoffmeyer wound things up. 'All right. I'd like more work done on this. I agree about Italy. Italy's out. We're talking Germany and the UK. Jack, I'd like to see more on costs, timings, impact of this new employment legislation the personnel team mentioned. Tom, come back with a clearer view from Marketing – current penetration by product by value by sector, like-for-like potential Germany versus the UK. Anything else you think is important.'

He turned to Brewster. 'Nick, get one of your people over to the UK. Go yourself, talk to the Government. Tell them we've got the biggest M and D facility this corporation has ever built, to put into Europe. Tell them Germany's the front runner but we're looking for a reason to build in the UK. Make clear what this could mean for them in jobs, exports, technology transfer, all of it. Make clear we'd look for a smooth entry, no problems, no small print. Lay it all out. Make them understand we're looking for co-operation.'

It was not until Brewster had got through to London and spoken to the Minister's office and the surveyors were packing up for the day at Stinston Bridge that the old man noticed the silt behind the island and the white rings around the three old posts. It was only when he turned on the news that night that he realized just how dry the winter had been.

Year 2, March

The heron in the beech tree felt it first. He had been watching the fox trotting by the Oak Stream, following the line of scent that the rabbit had left, when the branch beneath him moved. It was as though he had been standing on a sleeping creature that had stirred. The heron half-lifted his wings, took his weight on the air, regained his balance and settled again. The branch eased forward and back.

Upstream, the sky was as clear and blue as it had been all winter. Overhead, two ostrich plumes of cloud, high and thin, were reaching forward. There were more high clouds behind them, flat and white. Downstream, the clouds were low and bruised. Rain was hanging under them like torn rags.

The heron felt another breath and the rushes shivered. A duck flew upstream like an arrowhead homing. The moorhen that had been under the tree at Top Bend ran back to her nest, her head tilted forward and her long legs striding, her feet leaving a chain of rings ebbing out.

When it came, the rain advanced up the valley like a grey wall. It seemed to fall in single pieces, smacking and thwacking. Then it drummed and roared. In no time it was cascading from the farmhouse gutters and leaking through the crack above the door to the stalls. The cattle on Five Acre stood in conference and endured it. The mares kept their heads down but it seeped into their eyes.

The rain that fell all day and almost all night and part of the next day ran down the wooded slopes and gathered at the bottom. It ran from one hollow to another and joined them up. The Tussock Stream and the Oak Stream and the Barn Stream turned brown. The grannom fly behind the island was crucified on an eddy and drifted in circles with her legs hanging down.

The trout that the kingfisher had scarred felt the water lift and its lightness go. He felt a low strength rising and an unsettling push. The trout edged nearer the bank and hugged the bottom. The mayfly nymph beneath him backed down her burrow and lay still. The patch of chokeweed that had held on all winter at Middle Bend lifted and turned downstream, dark as an old coat. The willow tree behind the Otter Stone fell into the water when the bank beneath it collapsed.

When the stream flooded Hinters it raced straight for the mole's tunnel and headed down it. The push of air in front of it seized the mole's brain and held him; then the water rushed up behind him and caught and consumed him in a torrent of mud and dust and grass and seeds and small stones and cockroaches and ants and half-eaten worms and his own dried droppings. It pushed and bundled him until he wedged at the place where the big stone jutted out and the claws of his foot became trapped in the root. The mole struggled briefly then he hung there limply, jostling and swaying with his eyes wide open and his throat clogged up.

So much rain fell on the day that Nick Brewster had lunch with the Minister's number two and the day after that when he met the officials, that all work on marking out the route of the road had to stop.

Then the sun came back just as hot as before. By the time the first of the swallows was lifting and soaring and sculpting the air, the stream was no higher than it had been since the summer and the white rings were showing again around the three old posts.

Year 2, April

It was in the week when the city of workmen's cabins was completed at Stinston Bridge that it arrived. In some ways, the old man thought, it was worse than if it had come out of the blue. At least if something came out of the blue it was because you had no inkling of it before. But, of course, he had known there was a problem. He had tried to push it to the back of his mind but little by little it crept further to the front. A bit like a gathering storm, really. Like that or an illness. At first, nothing. Then a change, a change so subtle that by the time you realized it was there you knew it had been there a while. You tried to ignore it or hope it would go away. Some symptoms and omens. A low gnawing, maybe. Or a sudden stab of pain. Diagnosis.

That was how it had all built up. For years, everything had chugged along. Then things were OK, then a bit of a struggle, then a worry. Costs up, income down. Making do. Suddenly patching and fixing. Putting off till next month when that cheque comes in. The roof, the tractor, the ditches. The land itself.

Pressure from his son. Worst of all, pressure from his son because there was no escape from that.

Now the letter. The old man read it again, pulled the drawer open and pushed the envelope to the back. A warning, however he read it. He would have to answer it sooner or later but he could hold out for a while. Which, of course, he would do. To the very last minute. To the very last second. No, the bank could wait.

Year 2, May

It was a tiny movement, a tease in his eye, a smudge on his vision, no more. The trout that the kingfisher had scarred whirled, curved himself so that the current swept him downstream and then edged forward. He saw the movement again and stopped, riding the water like a sleek, tethered kite, lifting and sliding, soaring and dipping. The puffs of silt were rising behind the flat stone, lifting like signals as though to attract him. The trout moved nearer. He saw the burrow in the stream bed and the mayfly nymph in its entrance. He saw her edge forward as if to emerge and then suddenly retreat. Another puff of silt she had distributed, drifted out. The trout turned on the water, edged downstream again and approached at a shallower angle. In the time the small movement took, the mayfly nymph seemed to throw all caution aside. She braced her legs against the burrow entrance, pushed hard behind her and scrambled out.

The nymph moved cautiously at first and then more quickly, darting about the stream bed between the clusters of silt and fragments of weed with an urgency that could almost have been taken for excitement. It was as if she were enjoying the novelty of space and the captivation of freedom when the trout tilted down and took her.

The mayfly nymphs hatched in ones and twos after that. The trout with the scar took several behind the round stone he had won and several more from behind his flat stone and two more as they left the stream bed behind the big stone he now hid under when danger threatened.

Not long after the trout with the scar managed to avoid the stab-stab-stab of the heron's beak by frenziedly twisting this way and that, on the same day that the bale-eyed pike had two more goes at him, nymphs began to leave the stream bed to hatch in procession. The mayflies lifted into the radiant emptiness above them while the buttercups opened and the hawthorns unfurled their lace and the first borehole was being sunk in the search for water.

It was on the day that the old man took the letter from the bank from the back of the drawer and read it through slowly several times before returning it that the hatch of mayflies reached its peak. By the time the drilling had to stop for the day and the water caterpillars were on the move again and the salmon that had been singled out by the Clearwater from far away had been singled out by the stream and was settling into the deep pool beneath the kingfisher's nest, the stream was filled with nymphs swimming upwards beyond numbering and the air was filled with hatched flies beyond numbering.

All the little trout that lived in the shallows above Top Bend and downstream from the falls and in the riffling water below the spawning gravels in each of the streams that crossed the meadows to the west, fed on the hatching mayflies until they could feed no more. The big trout on the outsides of all the bends where the currents funnelled flies into their waiting mouths, gorged. The dark nose of the great fish close to the bank by the island, the one that lay behind the projecting root and that had owned that place since the drought had begun, made rings on the surface among the floating flies without ending. Even the weak fish that had been driven away to the least good places by fish that were stronger and more determined, eased the aches in their guts. Only the blind fish near the place where the bear's skull had lain buried so long and the old fish that had buried itself in the weed alongside Picket Close to die, missed out. On the day after the Department of Transport and Industry issued its reminder that the Broadchalk and the Clearwater rivers were to be protected absolutely and the search for piped water was moved even further away to make sure that they were, the mayflies were dancing so densely on the air that their wings gauzed the sun. The swifts were screaming and the swallows were swooping. The old man was looking at it all and rejoicing. The great fields on the high hills were being sprayed again.

Year 2, June

The caterpillar on the plant behind the trout with the scar was a great caterpillar. He was at least as long as the hyphens in the letter the old man had received from the bank. He moved with that curious, high-stepping walk that some caterpillars have, drawing his body up into a loop and reaching forward, then looping and reaching again.

Each time he moved, the grub of the little black fly that the old man would have called a caterpillar if he had seen it because he called any grub a caterpillar if it looped and reached, laid out the safety line that the law of continuing had given him. He had already used the line twice in emergencies, each time when one of the furnace-eyed caddis grubs had crept along the plant he was holding and lunged. Both times he had let go of the plant and the current had plucked him away and the silken thread had tethered him in the water far out of danger, exactly as the law of continuing had intended. Both times when the caddis grubs had seemed to tire of waiting and had gone away hungry, the caterpillar that was at least as long as a hyphen in ordinary-sized typescript had wound in the line again and hauled himself back to safety.

It was on the day that work started on Stinston Bridge and the *Financial Times* reported that Cogent Electronics and Top Oil were on the point of signing for sites on the development that the caterpillar that lived by catching food from the current, moved a long way down his plant.

He laid out a lot of line and covered a great distance, perhaps the width of a small trout's tail, before he found a place on the plant where he could get all the food he wanted. When he found the place he took a firm hold and settled there.

The caterpillar had moved further out from the base of the plant because of something the law of continuing had told him. The law of continuing had told him that the slower the water flowed the less the plant would move and the less the plant moved the less water he could be swept through and the less water he was swept through, the less food he was likely to catch. It was because of this that the water caterpillar moved further down the crowfoot plant: this and the fact he had been told the fastest-moving parts of any plant at any time were its extremeties; this and the fact that the current had begun to slow in a way that only a water caterpillar and some of the nymphs that lived on stones and a few others could detect.

By the time the sun was setting and Jim Hampton of Hamptons was suddenly realizing just how hard the new Asian imports were hurting his business, the caterpillar that lived by panning and fishing was covering much more water. By the time the sun had set he had already caught one of the cells of chokeweed that the trout with the scar had displaced with his tail.

Year 2, July

The salmon that settled into the deep pool beneath the kingfisher's nest at Bottom Bend lay close to the stream bed, scarcely moving.

He had been a year in the seas to the north and west, harrying the little fish that hung in chain-mail curtains; then there had come an emptiness inside him for all he had eaten, a hunger as though for food but not for food and he had headed south again.

The salmon that had left the stream as a little fish and was returning as a great fish had stayed close to the coast when he neared it. He had passed the salmon farm in the bay where the tame fish in the cages were fed on wild fish that had been caught and ground down and processed and pressed into biscuits. He had passed the ship that had its holds full of wild fish on their way to power stations where they would be burned as fuel because they were so cheap and the other ship that had its hold full of wild fish on their way to be turned into fertilizer for spreading on the land. He had passed the ship that was flushing oil from its tanks where no-one could detect it and the nets that had broken away from trawlers so that they drifted like shrouds, catching fish to no purpose.

The salmon that had left the stream a year before had still been far out to sea when he smelled the familiarity in the water and the scents of the Broadchalk began to gather him to them. He had reached the place in the estuary where the car ferries chuntered and the bright dinghies bounced and the water patted and lapped against their hulls before the scents of the Clearwater singled him out. He had passed the place where the plastic bags tumbled and the flat fish shuffled like stones over the bottom before he glimpsed the fleeting light and saw here and gone and here again the images of the golden gravels and the swaying plants and the caddis grubs crawling and the mayfly nymphs darting that the law of continuing put into his head as an enticement.

The salmon had stayed a week in the estuary of the Broadchalk River, drifting in and out with the tide while his body was made safe to move from salt water to fresh water and then he swam forward again. He swam without stopping under the road bridge that carried three lanes of traffic each way and leapt the leap in Farley while the visitors gasped and the cameras clicked.

Only when the braids of the Broadchalk loosened

and he found the Clearwater River did he slow. Only when he had swum up the Clearwater to the deep water opposite the place where the stream came in, did he rest. And then, on one of the days when the fields on the high hills were being sprayed with water and fertilizers again and the dust was rising over the earth-works beyond Stinston Bridge again and a borehole was being sunk in search of a water supply that would meet the demands made by the Minister and Cogent Electronics, he crossed the Clearwater like a grey shadow sidling and entered the stream that had given birth to the images he could see in his head.

The salmon that settled into the deep pool below the kingfisher's nest at Bottom Bend and who had been told that he would not eat again before spawning because no salmon that entered a river ate again before spawning, did not move until the feather that the cygnet had lost, drifted over him. He rose from the stream bed into the light and touched the feather with his nose because of the pictures of flickering mayflies it created in his head; but then he saw the falsity and the pointlessness of it all and sank to the bottom again to wait and the world closed over him.

Year 2, August

Another row. Well, not a row exactly, they both always tried to keep it this side of a row. Another heated discussion about the farm, anyway.

He had never understood his father. The two of them were like chalk and cheese. His father still got excited when he saw an owl or an orchid or when the mayflies hatched. His father still talked about the salmon in the stream as 'the secret'. Amazing the difference a generation made. And an education. Odd, though. Odd that as a lad with a father like that he should have been interested in a farm as a farm and not as a great place to play.

His own friends had been surprised at him, as well – not that there had been many of those, stuck out here. As a boy he'd even played farms. 'I'm going to grow this here and that there. The other will grow better if we do so-and-so. No, it's worth more than that, mister, I've worked hard to grow it.' It had set the pattern for a lifetime. A farm was a business was a business. Might as well build on it if it's not producing. Or lay a golf course.

Interesting he'd turned out that way, though. Maybe his father had just pushed him too hard. Even after a long day in the fields Dad would come back and insist on taking him to see something he'd found. Interminable walks. 'Look at this, look at that. See the other, see it, see it? Look at the way this . . . Isn't that wonderful, isn't the other amazing?' Isn't it boring. His father not just showing him but demanding a reaction, requiring an enthusiasm to match his own. Maybe that was what had made him the way he was. Force-feeding. Overdose.

The young man had crossed Foremeadow and Aftdown and Penny Furlong before he realized where he was. He stopped on Barrows, just downstream from the falls, and looked around, idly tossing a stone from hand to hand.

What a mess. The house in a state, the barn roof loose, the tractor on its last legs – well, wheels. And the land! Ditches clogged and overgrown, hedges out of control, pretty well all the land along the lower stream tussocked and useless. It didn't have to be like this. This drought wasn't going to last for ever and there was so much that could be done. The new drainage techniques he'd read about could make a big difference, a huge difference. The hedges taken out so the fields could be made a workable size. Some treatment with those new compounds. Some of the modern hybrids planted. The subsidies and grants to take the pain out. New equipment with the easier loans – the place could be transformed. Would his father listen? Would he!

The young man lobbed the stone into the stream as he turned and headed back. He didn't notice where the stone landed, or see the little fish it crushed and stunned or see the whole packed shoal burst into a thinned circle around the empty place where the stone went in and where the dark clouds lifted and the water fizzed.

He didn't notice the joyous bellyflop his young dog made when it retrieved the stone, or see the white bellies that winked or the mouths that stayed open or the eyes that stared when the dog had gone back to him barking and jumping.

The tiny fish that had felt the pain and then no pain, the fry that had her back broken when the stone landed on her, was caught on the surge of water the dog sent out and was carried away on the current.

When the stream had tumbled her over and over so that there were in her world only slabs of light and slabs of dark; after it had turned her slowly on the eddies and spun her on the whirlpool; after it had drifted her belly-up and twitching across the stream from the high bank where the martins nested to the shallow water on the other side, the trout with the scar that owned that place angled his fins and slid a little to one side and accepted her.

It seemed a long time after the trout with the scar had taken the little fish and met his own needs of the moment and after the young man walking the fields with his own needs and dreams had moved away, that the last of the dark silt in the empty place settled.

Year 2, September

The great fish that the otter chased had escaped from the trout farm on the Clearwater River in the flood.

The Clearwater had risen just as the stream had risen and it had washed over the flat land into the ponds where the little farmed trout were kept and fed and the fish had been swept into the river like spilled silver coins.

Then the floodwater had washed over the grass to the pools where the medium-sized trout were being fed until there were precisely so many of them to the pound and kilo before they were killed and these fish were washed into the river as well.

As the mole was drowning in his tunnel under Hinters, the waters of the Clearwater washed over the gravelled track where the great refrigerated lorries came and went each week and poured into the pools where the big farmed trout were kept for breeding.

It was the largest of all these trout that the otter chased. The trout had lived in the Clearwater ever since the flood, taking the feeding places of any fish she chose because the special biscuits she had been fed on at the farm had made her awesome and immense. She was three times bigger than the wild trout that had lived on what the river alone could provide, the one that owned the place where the bank jutted out just upstream from the farm. She was more than three times bigger than the trout that owned the big stone directly opposite, the one that had also had to feed on what the law of continuing had decreed should be adequate. The great trout from the farm was so big that no wild fish could resist her when she wanted its space and the food that space carried.

When she drove away the great wild trout from the place where the bank jutted out, that fish drove away the fish behind the stone and took its place and the fish behind the stone drove away a fish that lived nearby and took that place. All the way up the river and down, all of the fish that had escaped from the trout farm in the flood drove the wild fish away from the lies the law of continuing had said they should have and those wild fish drove away smaller fish of their own kind to make spaces for themselves.

Every move was a bad move for the wild fish because each fish was driven from a place that had proved adequate to its needs to a place that only had enough food passing through it to sustain something smaller. Even the largest of the escaped trout grew thinner because the farm food had made them bigger than any fish the law of continuing had meant the river to feed.

Around the time the water caterpillar was on the move again, the great trout that the otter was to chase was already feeling the cramps in her gut. Around the time that the salmon returning from the sea was settling into the deep pool beneath the kingfisher's nest at Bottom Bend, the coarse flakes of flesh along the great trout's flanks showed like ridges under her skin. By the time Ethical Pharmaceuticals had announced its intention to take the site between Cogent Electronics and Top Oil and the new bridge at Stinston had been completed and the young man was lobbing his stone into the stream and breaking the little fish's back, the great farmed trout was lean and dark and the changes that the law of continuing required of her, had begun.

The law of continuing that made demands on farm fish just as it made demands on fish in the river, drew out what goodness remained in her body and filled the slack cavities inside her with eggs, then it moved her to the place on the Clearwater where the stream entered and sent her up it.

She passed the coot's nest under the old bridge on Longate on the same day that the Phase One road was completed and she reached the three old posts opposite the swans' nest around the time the young protesters were deciding to dig tunnels to slow the advance of the bulldozers. She lay for a long time in the pool close to the fallen willow and all the fish there were displaced downstream by one.

The trout with the scar had felt the same panic as the little fish when the great farm trout shrugged her way

87

from the quiet pool by the fallen willow to the lit shallows of the Cattle Drink. He had seen the little fish dashing and winnowing upstream past him, seeking places to hide under the plants and stones. The trout with the scar slid softly as a shadow away to allow the great fish through, watching her all the time. The farmed trout passed the place that the trout with the scar had left and hesitated by the stones with the little fish under them, jostling head-down and feeling safe though their tails were in the open and waving like fringes of weed.

For a long time the great fish idled near the high bank by the place where the sand martins nested before driving herself forward to the shallows beneath the falls. The farmed trout had no mate but still the law of continuing demanded she do what she could. It seized her and made her roll onto her side and thrash about but gave her no high note and no bright light to help her. She squeezed and contracted without a mate to stroke her and a few loose eggs spilled out.

The otter that sometimes used the stream saw the commotion from her stone. She melted into the water and swam close to the bank, pushing a bow wave across the Cattle Drink and streaming bubbles behind.

By the time the foundations of the next part of the new road had been dug and the old man who could not bear the thought of change had argued with his son again, the great trout's scales were drying on the Otter Stone and the otter that had left them had gone.

By the time the foundations for the Cogent Electronics site were being laid and the old man had received the new letter from the bank and the otter and the trout had both gone, the brown line had come.

It ran along the water's edge down both sides of the stream. It ran past the willowherb and the purple loosestrife that were drooping. It ran past the places where the chokeweed was gathering. It ran past the Cattle Drink where the mud on the bank was baked as hard as stone and pitted with the impressions of remembered hooves.

The brown line, thin as a ribbon, wound around the water's edge from the place where the springs gathered behind the farm. It wound around the curves of Top Bend and Middle Bend and all around the island and along the banks on either side of the trout with the scar and past the place where the fallen willow hinged in the water. It wound above the head of the salmon that lay close to the stream bed with the world closed over him and around the shingle banks and along Picket Close and Longate past the coot's nest, all the way to the Clearwater. It wound all along the Clearwater to the Broadchalk and along the Broadchalk to the sea.

Year 2, October

When Simon Goode, the biologist, had told the inquiry
of his fears for the Broadchalk and the Clearwater if
they were abstracted or polluted, he had several times
mentioned the nymphs that lived on stones. From the
side or the front the 'stoneclingers', as he sometimes
called them, looked as if they had been designed in a
wind tunnel. They needed to be that way, he said,
because of the niche they filled.

The small, smooth, grey stone exactly one-third of
the way across the stream and directly in line with the
rusted hinges on the door of the wooden hut, had once
been the perfect place for a stoneclinging nymph
because the water sleeking over it had been exactly the
right speed and depth. Even though the currents raced
and roared like a heavy wind above the stone and

looked strong enough to sweep anything on the stone away, the law of continuing had taken every generation of nymphs that had ever lived into account. The law of continuing had decreed that no matter how fast a current was, there should always be a place close to the stream bed where the water was slow. It had decreed this in the same way it had decreed that no matter how strongly the wind blew, there should always be less wind near the ground. The law of continuing had decided the two things together because they were so closely related.

And so right on the bed of the stream, immediately above each stone and grain of held sand and piece of lodged shell and over all the depressions between them like a thin lain sheet, there was a space between the roaring current and the stock-still stones where the water moved slowly. The space was about a nymph's height high, scarcely deeper than the smallest print in the agreement that the old man had signed with the bank. Because the law of continuing had created a niche for everything and put everything into its niche, it had shaped some nymphs to live and cling on there.

Because she had been designed for that space, the body of the stoneclinger on the small, smooth, grey stone was sleek and her head was low and her legs were braced out to either side to hold her stable. And so the nymph on the small, smooth, grey stone lived in comfort under the current that raged overhead and that looked as though it should be sweeping her away.

She had known of the changes in the water before the salmon had returned. She had almost been hit when the silt particle crashed down like a boulder near her head and she had long known of the cord of chokeweed that had taken hold beside her. She had felt the thin, lain sheet of water growing steadily thinner and the turbulence above it reaching down to unsteady her.

It was on the day that the young protesters in the tunnels began to worry about suffocating in the heat, just about the time Jim Hampton of Hamptons was warning his workforce there would have to be cuts if the business were to be saved from the cheap Asian imports, that the stoneclinging nymph on the small, smooth, grey stone began to edge sideways. She lifted her right foreleg and right hindleg and left middle leg all at the same time and reached them as far to her right as she could, traced and groped for a footing for each of them and set them down. Then she reached her left foreleg and left hindleg and right middle leg over to follow them. She repeated the movement again and again, all the time keeping a grip with three legs to keep herself stable, all the time keeping her sleek, sloping head into the current so the water could not reach under her and sweep her away. She moved right across the small, smooth, grey stone and down its side and up the side of the rough stone next to it and across the top of that stone and down its side and up the side of the stone beyond that and across it. She kept moving even after the rope of chokeweed had snaked around her left foreleg and she had to pull and tug and back a little downstream and pull and tug again before she could get herself free.

The stoneclinging nymph was five stones further out towards the middle when she settled. The water that had once been too deep for her there was now the right depth and the thin layer of slow water there that had once been wrong for her was now right.

All the nymphs that lived on stones opposite the wooden hut moved further towards the middle about the same time and so did the grubs of the brown-winged caddis flies near the place where, in ancient times, the elk had stumbled on his way to drown in the swamp. The nymphs of the dainty Baetis flies followed suit. The water caterpillar near the trout with the scar, the one that had already reached and looped the length of five grown mayflies along its strand of water crowfoot, looped further towards the end soon after.

The trout with the scar rose up in the water and flared his gills about the same time and drove away the sick trout that had lived nearer the middle and that had no energy left for fighting. The trout with the scar took the place nearer the middle that he needed because the water in his old place had been growing shallow and he lifted and slid and forged and swirled, enjoying the plenty that had been sent there to feed him.

In the week David Hoffmeyer decided he would look at the new site when he was in the UK next and the trout with the scar moved, it seemed as if all life in the stream was on the move. It seemed as if every creature that relied on current had decided to edge towards the middle and that the silt in the margins was in pursuit.

Year 2, November

'You'll soon see what I mean.' Paul Tyler had to shout to be heard. The helicopter was beginning to vibrate. The noise that had begun as a click and a whine rose to a roar. The yellow tips of the rotor blade blurred a circle around them. Johnson and the others on the ground backed away, shielding their eyes from the dust. The helicopter lifted like a gigantic gnat, stood on its nose and turned.

David Hoffmeyer peered down and nodded. It was a big development all right. And things were much further advanced than he'd expected.

Tyler half-turned to face him. 'We've had a fraction of the rain we usually get. Very little last winter. It's winter rain that fills up the ground around here so the water table stayed low and gave us a flying start on the footings.' Tyler pointed to the sun blazing above the canopy. 'Then a bone-dry summer. Forecast is for a second dry winter. We'll break all records at this rate. If the protesters let us, that is.'

The helicopter headed up the Broadchalk valley, along the line of the Phase One new road. The concrete strip was lined with lorries travelling in a near-unbroken chain, each way.

'The protesters are a bit of a problem. They slow things up, which is what they want. We've had to go to court three times, so far. They've got some heavy-duty lawyers helping them. You couldn't buy the advice of some of their lawyers, but a couple of the best will work for nothing on something like this.'

Hoffmeyer nodded. 'Show me the site.' He didn't like helicopters much. He didn't like having to shout much, either. In an aircraft, if you got in front of the engines, noise was no problem. In a chopper the rotor was right over your head.

Tyler tapped the pilot on the shoulder, leaned over and pointed. The helmeted head nodded. Tyler had been Whole-site Director from the start and right now things were as busy as they could be. Still, if somebody like Hoffmeyer wanted thirty minutes of your time, you gave it. It had been the Ministry that had put the request through.

'The Clearwater.' Tyler indicated to his right. 'Beautiful. Pristine. The only development on the whole river is a fish farm, believe it or not. Great land, very productive. Hence the size of the fields.' He smiled, half-apologetically. 'They're big for us.'

The view directly beneath them was the one several

newspapers had photographed. There had been a purple piece in the *Guardian*. He could remember the first paragraph because the cutting was on his notice-board. It ended with something like '. . . gouged earth, shattered trees, blue smoke billowing up from the fires. Cables and pipes, concrete and steel, trenches and mounds. Everywhere the roar of engines and the pounding of piledrivers, the swirling dust and the baking heat. It looks like the ending of the world'. Something like that, anyway.

The woman from the *Telegraph* had taken a different approach. That's why the two cuttings were side by side, to show how differently two people could view the same event. He could remember some of her first para-graph verbatim, no problem. It ended: 'This is human endeavour on an heroic scale. This is what it must have been like when they were building the pyramids.' Personally, he didn't see it either way. Still, you pays your money and you takes your choice. So long as the job gets done.

'The new bridge. There's the old one beyond it. Your site is further up. Biggest of the lot.'

'Ninety acres,' Hoffmeyer shouted. 'Ten acres of buildings, Stage One. More later. We'll landscape the rest – water gardens, walks, that kind of thing. We'll give the public some access. We always do. Helps local relations.' Tyler nodded. He knew. And it was ninety-two acres, not ninety.

Hoffmeyer was still looking down, having to shout. 'We'll be putting a brand-new technology in here. We're going to be manufacturing here for Europe and the Middle East. There'll be a development lab as well.'

A few moments later, Tyler pointed straight ahead. 'Those are the Hangers. That's the Frontage on the right.' Hoffmeyer had heard of both already. Brewster had mentioned the protests about them in one of his reports. Then there had been that guy in the airport lounge in Boston. He'd been a pain in the neck, going on about some 'Shrinking Planet' article in the *New York Times*. There had been a picture of Stinston and some demonstrations and a story saying how the Brits were in the front line of it all because the UK was so small but it would all be happening in the US before long. He'd gone on and on.

Tyler was saying something. 'The dark vehicles are police vans. They've put a cordon around the tunnellers to stop supplies getting in. The stuff that looks like flotsam caught in the trees is tree houses. Some of the protesters are living in the trees to stop them being felled.'

Hoffmeyer looked down. Same views as the Boston rambler, probably. Maybe not the guys in the trees down there but the well-heeled professionals who joined them at weekends. Wanted it all, but at no cost. More food, more comfort, more possessions, more territory so to speak. The human animal all over. But total unreality about the price. Everything had a cost. Every product needed materials and materials needed a process. Big processes needed space and fuel and consumed all manner of resources but they closed their minds to that. Reminded him of people who salivated over steaks but wouldn't think of the abattoir.

The helicopter banked to starboard and flew along the top of the Frontage. 'You were telling me how much water this new process of yours needs. You wouldn't think it from here, but water has given us one of our problems.' Tyler pointed to the Clearwater on the right and the Broadchalk glinting to the left. 'We've got to supply the entire development without taking a drop from either of the rivers, or from the springs that feed them. Outstanding wildlife and plants.'

He pointed past the pilot's head, to the left of some woods on the middle horizon. 'We've had to come much farther than we expected to make sure we do no harm to either. No harm to anything out here. The Broadchalk is fed from its west bank and the Clearwater is fed from the east. This central area is the one safe place. Quite a big pumping operation, but these hills get topped up every winter.' He smiled. 'Well, most winters.'

Hoffmeyer peered down at the parked vehicles and the mobile drills and the small figures moving between them. Tyler waved an arm to the right. 'I guess you know you're going to have to have your own dedicated supply because of this technology of yours. Sourced from over there, somewhere. Going to use enough water to supply a small town, your people say. We're having to cut a few corners to do it. Pressure from the Minister himself, someone said.' Hoffmeyer shrugged. 'OK. Let's go.'

The roar from the helicopter unfurled over the development as it headed back to base, but in the valley in the woods where the small stream flowed and where the heron standing in the Cattle Drink was shaking the chokeweed from his foot, the sound was scarcely audible and going in a different direction.

Year 2, December

It was, when they mated, as though the whole of their lives had been aimed individually to that one purpose alone, as though the law of continuing had decreed that they would find one another and use one another on that exact day, for all the intervening separation of their lives.

The cock salmon had been in the stream a long time before the hen had arrived and the law of continuing had gradually made him ready. It had worked on him all the time he had been in the pool under the kingfisher's nest at Bottom Bend and ever since he had moved up into the deep water close to the bank where the sand martins nested. All his gleaming silveriness had gone. The back that had once been as green as a high seas cavern, had darkened and dulled. His sides had become blotched with purples and reds. His skin had thickened and shrunken in on his skull and his lower jaw had turned up in a hook. His insides had filled with milt.

The hen fish had still been far along the coast when he was entering the Broadchalk. When he was turning from the Broadchalk into the Clearwater she had not even reached the place where the ferries chuntered or the water patted and lapped against the bright dinghies' hulls. It was long after he had swum past the fallen willow and since the trout with the scar had moved aside and let him through that she had leapt the leap in Farley while the visitors were gasping and the cameras were clicking and the little girl was letting her lollipop fall into the water.

It was only after the hen fish had turned aside from the Broadchalk into the Clearwater and from the Clearwater into the stream and had passed the fallen willow and the trout with the scar that the cock fish sensed her near. It was only when she eased into the dip in the stream bed a little further out from him and a little way downstream, that he knew she was there.

It was, when he saw her, almost as if he could not believe what he had seen. It was almost as though the salmon could feel inside him what in ancient times the man in the deer pelt had felt when he saw the girl whose smile was like the sun coming out. The cock salmon pushed with his tail and angled his fins so the water caught him and lifted him and he soared like a swallow over the hen fish when he reached her and then soared back. At once the hen fish lifted and soared in the water as he lifted and soared; and they swam around

101

and around in circles and upstream of one another and downstream of one another as though excited and knowing. They rode and soared and lifted like young things; and then they settled and lay side by side close to the stream bed while the law of continuing gripped their bodies and a bright light began to glow in the steel helmets of their heads.

The two salmon lay side by side in the pocket of deep water until the leaves on the beech trees were clinging as sparse as winter butterflies and Lisa Pearce had got the funding for her programme on climate change. And then, on the day when the first frost of winter closed its fist over the ground and the breath of the sleeping vole was hazing the air in his burrow, the hen salmon angled her fins and planed upwards and outwards until she could feel the draw of the current and the cock salmon moved upwards and outwards alongside her as though joined to her with strings.

The two of them, the hen salmon first and then the cock, eased their way beyond the place where the male trout from the three old posts was already waiting for a partner and past the eddy where the hen trout from near the coot's nest and the cock trout from the shingle banks were showing an interest in one another. They swam straight through the shallower water where the trout always spawned and moved into the deeper water near the falls where the salmon had been told to mate. They found a place there where the water was as deep as they were long and where the light slid and melted over the stones and golden gravel and played back the images they had long carried in their heads.

That first day it was as though the fish were enjoying

the familiarity and rightness of the place that the lights in their heads had brought them to, save for the silts that had settled there that had not been there before. On the second day while the cock fish whirled and snapped at the other males that tried to approach her and showed them his hooked jaw and teeth, the hen fish rolled onto her side close to the falls where no silt had settled and began to thrash down. The hen tested the gravels while the sun rose and fell, her body arching and driving, the water pushing and welling, the stones lifting and floating behind her.

On the morning of the third day, before the cock could crow or the heron could shake his feathers or the sun could touch the rim of the tunnel where the vole lay sleeping, the hen settled into a scoop that she had made and felt it right and the cock fish moved up beside her and felt it right. Then the law of continuing touched them and the bright light that had aimed each of them there drew in on itself and grew brighter and brighter and resolved to a piercing point that seized and held and made a high note; and the cock fish trembled and the hen fish shook and the eggs streamed and the milt flowed and the eggs streamed and the milt flowed and the eggs and the milt flowed and flowed.

Year 3, January

It was almost as though the plan had been mislaid.

The plan for the springs had always been that they would flow strongly in winter, but after two parched summers and coming on for two dry winters the springs were lower in winter than at any time in the old man's lifetime. The plan for the stream had always been that it should be running fast and deep in winter, but after two parched summers and coming on for two dry winters the trout with the scar and his mate had to look hard to find any water at all that was fast enough for spawning.

The plan for the plants could almost have been forgotten. The plan for the water crowfoot had been that it would thrive in the kinds of places where fast water had been decreed, yet everywhere that fast water had been the water crowfoot was beginning to die for want of flow. The plan for the slow-water plants was that there should be few of them anywhere yet everywhere slow-water plants were taking root.

It had certainly been the plan that there should be lots of insects in the stream, even if in winter they would mostly be only half-grown or hiding away and yet there were fewer nymphs and grubs and all the others because so many of them needed water crowfoot if they were to thrive and multiply and the water crowfoot was on the wane.

One thing that had seemed central to the plan was that there would be little chokeweed in summer and almost none in winter because the water would be too cold and fast, but matted clumps of chokeweed that had grown in summer were holding on wherever the trout with the scar and his mate looked for a place to spawn.

By the time the two fish were busy on the gravels and the silt that the hen fish disturbed with her digging was clouding the water and putting a catch in the gills of the fish digging behind, it seemed as though the law of continuing had forgotten the plans. Or perhaps was making others.

Year 3, February

Paul Tyler was just flicking through his diary to see what he could move to fit in a visit by the executive from Top Oil when the speck that had once been part of the chipped grey flint at Middle Bend drifted downstream and settled onto one of the eggs in the gravels that the trout with the scar had put a light inside.

David Hoffmeyer was just touching down in Boston feeling well pleased with himself and the deal in Beijing when what had once been part of the root of the alder leaning out over Top Bend settled onto a second egg.

The man from Gothenburg – the one who so admired England that he had decided to spend all his holidays there from now on – was just going to bed and the Japanese who had been near him while the Minister was making his statement were all just getting up, when

106

a minuscule piece of the old tile on the stream bed opposite the farm and the tiniest fragment of wood from the jammed branch upstream of the place where the salmon rode and soared and lifted like young things, settled onto the third egg one after another.

By the time a dark fleck was settling over the sixth egg, the young man was showing the old man the plans he had made for the farm and saying oh, by the way, he had found the letters from the bank at the back of the drawer.

By the time Nick Brewster was staring into the bottom of his glass in Buenos Aires on his fifth trip there in as many weeks and wondering what he was doing with his life and the old man was telling the young man he could not change the way he was and that he would hold onto the farm as it was until the last possible moment because once made the changes could never be unmade, the lights in many of the eggs that the trout with the scar had lit had been dimmed by the specks of shadows and gone out.

On the same day that the trout with the scar began to edge downstream towards the willow that had fallen in the flood, the pump was switched on. The column of water that was 55 metres high and a metre wide in the fold in the hills that was so far from the Broadchalk and the Clearwater that neither could possibly be affected by its loss, lifted smoothly up the borehole lined with concrete and steel and began its silent journey through the pipes.

Year 3, March

The young salmon that had hatched from the gravels near the lodged twig and the white stone was finding it difficult to win a place for himself. Every space that could sustain a salmon fry had a salmon fry in it and had been fought for and won.

The young salmon that was longer than the light switch on the bank manager's wall, maybe as long as the first joint on the finger the young man used to work his calculator, often rose up in the water and made his eyes blaze and opened his jaws so other fish could see how great and terrible they were, but he found that the young fish everywhere he went were just as big and terrible and needy as he was and they drove him away.

All during the time Jim Hampton of Hamptons was humming and hahing about the number of redundancies that would be necessary and the case of the last tunnellers was being argued out on a technicality in the courts at Farley, the young salmon was being driven from stone to stone and gravel patch to gravel patch, always further downstream and nearer the bank.

The place where he settled while the big demonstration was being planned by Jo Hamilton of SAVE and Peter Althorpe of One Earth was not a good place. It was not a good place even though that place had often sustained salmon before. Though the space was as big as a waterhen's wing, silt had filled in the spaces between the stones and joined them all up until the stream bed was as smoothed and raised as an upland plateau.

The stream was like this wherever any of the salmon fry went. Where once everything had been clean and clearly defined and the stones had risen like ridged mountain ranges above a young fish lying near the stream bed, the stones now lay beneath the silt like low, domed hills. Where once the high stones had hidden young salmon in the valleys between them so that each fry could not see the others and knew it owned the whole stream and all the food it carried, the salmon fry could now see one another whenever one dashed to the surface to snatch anything that could be eaten. Each fry when it saw another attacked it because the other should not have been there and one fry of the two was always driven away.

The young salmon that had hatched beside the lodged twig and the white stone lay in the space that was as big as a waterhen's wing from the day the last of the young protesters in the tunnel issued his defiant warning and said he would stay there for ever no matter what anyone did, until the day when the court gave its ruling and the police dug him out. That was the day when the salmon from beside the small, lodged twig and the round, white stone, saw the other salmon fry enter his space and attacked her.

The young salmon that was longer than the light switch on the bank manager's wall poured all his gathered energy into the rush across his space and he opened his jaws and flared his gills at the intruder. The law of continuing had told the little male fry that he could not afford to lose his space and the hen fry that she must win it and so when he flared his gills and opened his jaws so that the intruder could see how great and terrible they were, she did the same; and when each could see that the other was not to be frightened away the two fish twisted and turned and snapped and chased one another in tight circles so that the silt was lifted and the nearby leech drew into himself and the dead caddis grub that the wading cow had caught with her hoof, was briefly exhumed. The two fry fought until the cock fish that had been driven away from the place near the lodged twig and the white stone was exhausted and bitten on the tail and the side; and he left his space to the hen fish because he could fight no more.

The young cock salmon allowed the current to carry him downstream beyond the place where the choke-weed was growing as thick as fur and where the nymphs and shrimps and grubs were having to clamber over it or to force their way under it to get anywhere. He was pushed and harried downstream by other fry every-where he sought to rest. He was driven past the place where the water caterpillars were having to reach and grope like blind worms to find places where they could take a hold amid the flecks of shadows that were settling everywhere over the plants around them. He was bullied and jostled towards the bank where the seeds that had fallen onto the brown ribbon along the edge were beginning to split in their delineated places and to send down roots white as hairs and to push up shoots that stretched and unfurled as though awaking from a sleep so that the exposed silt could be claimed for the land. It was only when he came to the deep scoop close to the Otter Stone that nothing attacked him and he settled down into it among the other fry there. The defeated salmon fry all huddled together over the silt that half-filled the scoop, waiting for the food that the slowed current could not bring them and for the heron and the kingfisher to return.

Year 3, April

It took only a few minutes to put the development onto most television screens in the Western world. It took one five-hundredth of a second to put it onto every front page in Britain, onto the front page of *Le Figaro* in France, *Die Welt* in Germany and into the Foreign News pages of the *Washington Post*. The *Asahi Shimbun* ran the picture and an extended caption because the Osaka development had at last hit the headlines over there. The Prime Minister's office called for a briefing on the incident in case someone mentioned it at the Environment Summit.

Lisa Pearce had gone to cover the demonstration that SAVE and One Earth had organized on the approaches to the Frontage. So had Steve Jones, the staff photographer on the *Guardian* whose forte was finding the alternative view. The late, knotty obstacle dreamed up by Charles Cullinger QC, the civil rights activist, had been cleared out of the way at last. The work near the Frontage that had been stopped by the court so unexpectedly, had been given the go-ahead again.

The demonstration all looked pretty routine. There was the usual phalanx of security men and a scattering of police on one side and the usual motley collection of protesters, hopelessly outgunned in everything except conviction, on the other. It was precisely because the demonstration looked so routine that Pearce and Jones had broken away from the main site, to look for something different.

It all looked straightforward to Jo Hamilton and Peter Althorpe as well, at least at first. They both knew the real purpose now was not to save the Frontage or the Hangers – the last battle for those had been lost with the Cullinger hearing. The main purpose now was to keep the media interested and the development lobby on the hop. If enough fuss and public anxiety could be generated about this site – not about the development in principle because that would only alienate the public after the recession, but about the damaging way the plan had been tackled and in particular the absence of a tunnel – then maybe the Minister would give the next decision more thought and apply a different set of values to the one after that.

All the same, as with any crowd, there could be trouble. That was why Althorpe, when he mounted the stepladder and spoke, made the point about needing to avoid confrontation at all costs. Their sole aim was to show the public at large 'the real price they are paying for what they are getting – socially and culturally and environmentally,' he said.

By the time Lisa Pearce and Steve Jones had found their ways independently to the lower slopes of the Frontage where they could overlook the scene and put the whole thing into context – police, demonstrators, advancing machines, scarred ground, green fields, the part-completed buildings away in the distance – Hamilton was mounting the stepladder herself and getting her own wider view.

Same as usual. A few hundred, a thousand, who could really tell? Old, young and middle-aged, every class – amazing how things like this united people the way they did. Country jackets and ragged sweaters, cavalry-twills and torn jeans. Dreadlocks and ponytails and short-backs-and-sides. Tunnellers and tree people, weekenders from London. A couple of labradors on leads, some whippets on strings.

A few faces registered. Major Croft, crisp and upright and eighty if he was a day, there in the front as usual. Jane Sanderson's drop-out daughter, all earrings and metal and black. That woman she could never put a name to when they met, the one who kept writing letters to the *Herald*. The police inspector looking at the crowd looking at her. The odd, heavy silence the low murmuring made, nobody quite speaking out loud.

At the very moment the teams from Cogent Electronics and the Ministry started to discuss delivery dates for the products the Government had agreed to buy and the mayfly in its burrow near the island was casting its skin for the last time before hatching and Jo Hamilton was clicking on the megaphone to start speaking, it happened. One minute there was the sudden roar of engines from heavy earth-moving equipment to the left, then there was some shouting and part of the crowd surged forward, then the police vans were coming up the track from the Stinston road with wire mesh over their windscreens.

Pearce and Jones zoomed in their cameras from the hill. Neither noticed the lone figure away to the right, the figure in the white shirt holding the child by the hand, walking across the shattered earth. Nor had anyone else noticed until, a few minutes and five arrests later, there was a boom like an artillery gun as one of the earth-movers backfired and all fighting stopped and all eyes swung around.

'In all my years as a reporter, I have seen nothing more remarkable,' Pearce was to say on that evening's news. 'It was an act of folly, of courage, of gross irresponsibility, call it what you will – but on the edge of the battle that was raging a man in his late twenties, holding a small boy by the hand, deliberately put himself in the path of a line of vehicles that had broken away from the main convoy. Then he faced them head-on. Here is what happened next . . .'

She had been pleased with the pictures. Ken had done a good job. He had got it all. The lead vehicle was one of those huge, earth-moving machines. It was belching black smoke and roaring like a tank. A dozen other huge vehicles, all tracked like tanks, rumbled and roared behind it. The young man in the light trousers and white shirt with the little boy holding his hand, both of them looking pathetically slight, were dead ahead.

under one track drove towards the young man in the white shirt and the boy as if to force them to move, but the young man held his ground and the great machine stopped short, still roaring. It hesitated as if to go this way and that around him, and then headed to the young man's left. The young man took a few deliberate steps sideways, placing the boy and himself directly in its path, confronting it again. The huge vehicle stopped, hesitated a second time and then headed for the young man's right. The young man in the white shirt holding the child by his hand stepped sideways a second time and barred its way. Again the gigantic vehicle hesitated and turned and again the young man blocked its path and held his ground. It went on for a couple of minutes.

'Finally,' Pearce said over the pictures, 'the machine stopped and the engine died. There was a moment of complete stillness. It was as though the crowd and the police had been paralysed by fear of what might happen, or too fascinated by it to move. Then the police and some of the crowd ran to the young man and the boy and the rest of the crowd cheered.'

The next day all the papers were filled with images snatched from the television screen and reporting how Paul Chapman, 28-year-old father of two and Hero of Stinston, had been taken into custody and then released without charge. They all quoted the same words: 'I didn't really think at all. I just wanted to do something. I wanted to make a statement. I wanted my son to be a part of it. It's not just my world they're destroying here, it's his as well.'

Several of the overseas newspapers that used Steve Jones' syndicated shot quoted the *Guardian* editorial because it rang bells in their own countries. 'This one photograph says much about Western societies today,' the leader had said. 'In a single image we see man versus technology and human frailty versus brute force. We see the natural environment versus our hunger for material advancement. We all see questioned yet again our ability to define a future we will be able to live with – in every sense of that term.'

Even as the battle was being fought and the newspapers were being printed, the pump that was so far away from the Broadchalk and the Clearwater that it could do neither river any harm was being speeded up steadily. In the stream that was so far away it was beyond all conscious thought, the stoneclingers were edging sideways towards the middle again and the water caterpillars were reaching and looping further down their stems again and the trout with the scar was on the move towards the willow again to find deeper water.

Year 3, May

The old man had gone to the stream especially. He always tried to spend an hour there in late afternoon when the mayflies were hatching. The massed hatching of the mayflies, he often said, was one of the wonders of England's countryside. Some countries had their wildebeests and caribou and lemmings, we had the mayfly. The scale of its hatches, the suddenness and predictability of its appearances and departures, amazed him.

The great flies would hatch from the stream in numbers beyond imagining, but only for the last two weeks of May and maybe a couple of days in June. Then they would disappear until the same time the year after. Their appearance was so short, their disappearance so abrupt that by July it was easy to think they could have been an illusion. The flies were so long and so lovely, so elegant and slender, they reminded the old man of fairies or the ballerina he had seen on television that time, dancing Swan Lake.

The old man crouched down to watch as a mayfly close to the bank changed from a nymph to a fly. He saw the nymph that had just swum up from its burrow lie flat in the surface and strain and tremble. He watched as the skin along the nymph's back split and a great fly with wings emerged from the skin of its old self that had no wings and the old man marvelled at the sight of it as he always marvelled.

Her body was an inch long, the colour of ivory and arched delicately upwards. Her three tails were as long again, as fine-drawn as eyelashes and just as curved. Her wings were an inch tall and hazed with green. They were the shape of chapel windows and held nearly as upright. The old man followed the drifting fly downstream, saw her carried towards the willow that had fallen in the flood and a trout slash at her and miss and then she was gone.

The mayfly that the old man had watched flew towards the bank and then aimed for the elder bush. She avoided the web that was trembling with bodies and flew in through a gap in the leaves and branches. She grasped the first leaf that was unoccupied and hid under it.

There were mayflies everywhere in the bush, clinging under leaves high above ground exactly as the law of continuing had instructed. The law of continuing had written that mayflies should not eat or drink after leaving the water and had told them they would need to stay out of the sun to avoid dehydration. This was why all the flies knew to hide away under leaves, in the shade. It was because the law of continuing had also told them about the frosts that the flies knew to choose leaves high above the ground, where a frost could not strike up at their soft bodies in the night. It was because they were following the plan so long ago written that the mayflies were where they were.

The mayfly that the old man had watched did not move once she had settled. She did not move even though a loud cheer went up at the development because the shell of the main Cogent Electronics building had just been completed. She did not move even when the sun began to fall and the green light that filtered through the leaves began to mellow. She did not move even when the mayflies that had already been there a night and a day and that were ready to mate, fluttered back out of the bush into the open. She did not move even when darkness fell and some of the parts for the production line were unloaded under floodlights at the docks.

It was long after dawn, when the sun was lifting and the space in the bush was becoming suffused with green light again that the mayfly felt a warmth reaching through her. It was long after dawn when she felt the first of the soft, low clicks that the law of continuing sent every mayfly before ridding it of the last skin it would shed and the fly was made ready to mate.

About the time the first nymphs of the day were beginning to hatch in the stream and the spiders in their charnel houses were turning and bundling again, the clicks and pressures the mayfly had felt steadily rising began to quicken and gather and converge into one. And then the mayfly that had waited so long felt the hot rush inside her and the law of continuing come. The law of continuing reached into her far extremities and drew all her strings tight. It made her back arch and strain so that she might have heard it arching and straining and then her blood roared and a red light flooded through her head and fined to a fine point until it snapped and the skin of her back broke open and she arched and trembled and strained and pulled herself upwards and outwards and free.

When it was over, when the crusts of the earth had stopped splitting and roaring and falling away all about her, the mayfly that the trout with the scar had tried to get as she lifted from the surface, settled beside a husk of her old self for the last time. Her tails were longer and more finely drawn and her wings sparkled like water catching the sun.

As afternoon passed and the sun got lower and the shadows within the bush angled and tilted again, the wings of all the mayflies that were to mate that day began to open and close and glisten and wink. The males left first. One by one they began to rustle and flutter like trapped birds under the leaves, catching wing against wing and wing against leaf; and then in ones and twos and dozens they flickered up into the beams of light that slanted down through the bush and aimed for the brilliance outside.

The males gathered behind the bush and formed a dense cloud. They flew upwards and floated down-wards, flew upwards and downwards, rising and falling as though singing a high chorus. It was the same behind the broken willow and the alder and the hawthorn heavy with blossom as white as snow. It was the same behind the sycamores and the chestnuts and the beeches and the oaks and the high, tangled hedgerows. The rising and falling of the male flies seemed to fill the whole valley: their rising and falling and their joyous, high song.

The mayfly that had left the stream while the old man was watching, waited for a long time after the last of the males had gone. Then she edged to the tip of the leaf that had kept her safe and lifted tremulously into the lightbeam where fine particles floated. She flew along the lightbeam to the way out it showed her and left.

The mayfly that the trout with the scar had failed to catch flew up into the radiance climbing higher and higher, as though being offered upwards to the singing of hymns. She was thrown aside twice when a swift dived close and made the air churn about her. She was twice brushed by wings that floated down like sycamore keys because the ivory bodies between them had been snapped out by beaks.

Then the mayfly that had come to that place from the fallen willow where the trout with the scar tried to get her, saw the columns of males rising and falling and seemed excited by their odours and overwhelmed by their song. She saw them flying upwards and floating downwards, flying upwards and floating downwards, glittering in the sun and luring her onward. She flew into the middle of them, shining and seductive, the full ripeness of her body heavy with needing, the delirium in the air softening that part of her where her eggs pressed most.

The males took her instantly, first one and then another clasping her tightly and pressing his abdomen to her; and then another and a fourth and a fifth took hold of her, so many males wanting her that she could not bear their weight and together they all fell into the grass.

Later, when the males had left and her body was bursting with ripeness, she lifted from the grass and picked up the scent of the stream again; made for its gleaming course again; and flickered past the hawthorn with its burden of blossom whiter than snow, past all the trembling webs where the spiders were bundling, far beyond the fallen willow that the chokeweed was exploring. Upstream from the Cattle Drink, close to the place where the trout always spawned but not as near to the falls as the salmon usually mated she began flying low, dipping her abdomen onto the water, dropping her eggs in clusters at a time.

As the mayfly dipped and pushed and the choke-weed cells responded to the warmth in the water that should not have been there and Jim Hampton of Hamptons was signing more redundancy notices, the current seized the grey eggs as they fell in clusters and chains and took them as though in collusion to the places that a mayfly's eggs needed to be.

When she was done, when the last of her eggs had dropped into the space near the willow where her own journey had begun, when she was drained and spent and could fly no more, the mayfly collapsed onto the surface as though her long dream was over. As the low rays slanted and her own light was ebbing, she twisted and writhed on the water and was carried to the place by the fallen willow where the rings of a feeding fish dimpled the surface. And there the trout with the scar tilted up and took her, as the plan had always required.

Year 3, June

The day after his father had been called to the bank the young man spread all his papers on the kitchen table and begged the old man to come and look at them again.

The old man listened again while the young man's finger traced the plan of the rough meadows and the tussocked fields and the young man talked again of the money to be made if only the land could be prepared in the new way and if the new strains of crops could be planted and the new fertilizers that had been developed were used.

The old man felt the pressure of the young man's ambition growing by the moment and he glimpsed in his mind here and gone and here again an image of a mayfly jangling in a web. It was as he was reminding his son of how long the farm had been in the family and how what his son wanted to do would change things for ever, that the nuclei in the long cells issued still more instructions.

Even as the old man was saying he would make a decision soon and his son was asking why he did not say never because that was what he really meant, the cells of chokeweed on the roots of the alder at Top Bend began dividing.

It was as the young man was slamming the door and walking out in frustration that the cells that had been instructed to rupture, burst open and the spores burst out.

Before the young man had crossed Foremeadow and The Close and Farfield and could turn back through Five Acre and Homefield, the two hairs that the law of continuing had given each spore had whipped and paddled and driven each spore to the place it needed to be and then settled it down.

Before the long day had ended and the old man had fallen asleep in his chair because he was so weary of arguing and worrying about money, the spores released from the chokeweed cells at Top Bend and Middle Bend and Bottom Bend and everywhere else, were beginning to grow in new places. The spores inhaled the richness that had been seeping into the springs because the fields on the high hills had been sprayed so often and the plants that liked slow water did the same.

In all the margins and on the insides of the bends and in the long, straight reach between Top Bend and Middle Bend and behind the island and downstream from the fallen willow and in the deep pool beneath the kingfisher's nest and along the wide reach between Picket Close and Longate, the chokeweed and the slow-water plants grew and rejoiced and slowed the water more and created the conditions needed for their own survival.

Year 3, July

The willow that had fallen in the flood had long since stopped hinging on the current. It lay diagonally downstream, still and heavy, forcing all the water the stream carried into a channel around its end. So much water was funnelled into the space between the end of the tree and the bank of Oak Meadow that the current there was fast and deep. Water crowfoot still grew there and was filled with food. A long line of fish lived in descending order of size downstream from the tree, as the law of continuing had instructed. They fed well on the flies that drifted downstream on the surface and on the nymphs and shrimps and larvae that the current carried towards them beneath the surface; but the big trout at the front fed best because he took what he wanted and the others got what was left.

The pike lived in the still water behind the willow, sometimes lying over the dark silt that camouflaged her so well, sometimes lying beneath the foliage that trailed from the branch because that hid her completely. She had plenty of food because of the queue of trout. The queue always offered her its next-best fish when she had taken the fish from the front, because the fish that were lined up in ascending order of size downstream shuffled up to fill the space.

There was never any consciousness or plan when the pike hunted. Every movement she made was the right movement to make, every line and drift she took was the right line and drift.

The heron saw the pike begin to move not long after the young man had replied to the advertisement to find out just how much a drainage system cost and after Jack Visconti had toured the new Cogent Electronics site in person to satisfy himself there could be no repeat of Milan. The pike had rested for days, slowly digesting; had stayed like a lain log on the bed of silt, unmoving. And then the heron saw the pike's eyes brighten and tilt; saw her fins begin a slow easing in the water; noticed the trailing edge of her tail begin to crinkle and flex.

The heron did not see the tension that seized the pike's body like a slow shock rising, but he saw the fins behind her head reach out and splay. He saw the pike's body bend on the still water and the small pieces of weed and old leaves and the dark detritus in the place where the great fish had lain so long begin to lift and tumble as though in slow-motion; saw the silt stir and loosen and the pike's aimed head move forward.

The pike took her familiar route, easing herself along close to the fallen willow and then turning towards the current and its line of food. She stayed close to the stream bed as she neared the trout, sliding forward like an aimed lance drifting; making herself a fact of the stream, another shadow only, a line on the bottom.

The pike was interested only in the fish at the head of the queue: the big fish that kept lifting on the current and sipping down the flies that had begun to hatch. The eyes of the pike were fastened onto that fish as hard as a sprung trap.

The pike used a patch of chokeweed as cover for the last short distance. It was when she was only twice her own length away that she stopped swimming and angled her fins and tail on the water and lay still, so that the current carried her into the open and faced her head-on, dark upon dark, a shadow upon a shadow.

The trout was high in the water lifting and sliding, taking flies from the surface. The pike was beneath him and could see his belly gleaming. The trout saw only the flickering wings that sailed towards him; was enjoying the excellence of his place out in bright water, far from the black water where an unease always troubled him.

The trout had taken all the flies he could eat when the unease touched his eye when it should not have touched his eye and made an edged nerve tingle. The rings on the surface were still ebbing above him and the last fly he had taken was still in his throat. He turned head-on to the shadow that troubled him but saw only the pike's jaws and the glaciers rending and the ravening rush begin.

The trout with the scar saw nothing from his place in the queue downstream. He saw only the swirl in the water and the panic of the other fish and the scales that had been rasped from the big trout's flanks winking past him on the current.

Later, when calm had returned and the silt had settled and the heron had gone; when the pike again rested like a lain log on the stream bed close to the bank and when the other fishes were shuffling up to take their new places in the queue, the trout with the scar edged up one position, also. The biggest trout in the queue, the one that had been second before, had moved forward to take the first position as the law of continuing had told him. It was a little downstream from the willow and a little in from the current; a little out from the line and drift that the pike always took.

Year 3, August

The man in the deer pelt had spent a long time looking into the fire on the night before he died. It was something he often did, sitting in front of the smouldering logs long after the world around him had darkened to smudges.

He had no fear of the shadows that danced and reared. He had learned not to be afraid of the wolves that prowled there or the bears that roared there or of the shufflings of the pigs in the nearby dusk. He knew the wolves and the bears would stay away from the firelight. He liked looking at the pictures the hot embers showed him because they reminded him of his day and often showed him his future.

There was, on the night before he died, nothing in the fire that seemed to show his future though he looked hard for signs of it in the embers and in the yellow, licking flames and in the gases that bubbled and wheezed from the ends of the logs.

There was much about the hunt, he could see all of that clearly.

Near the edge of the fire was one of the logs that stopped the embers spreading. The bark had lifted from it in the heat. Its crinkled edge, black against the brightness behind, showed the woods on the sky-line in that day's dawn. The long, curved strip of ash that had turned from orange to white was the big river below. Here and there in the hot breaths of the fire, shapes and colours changed and showed him the rest.

The small embers showed him the shapes of the round huts all about him and, in the wisps of ashes glowing and shimmering when the night airs touched them, he saw people moving. To the back of the fire, amid the group of sticks that leaned on one another like toppled trees, he could see the pig he had hunted that day, the axe in his hands, the pig's wide eyes, the pig's tongue lolling and dripping. To the right, in front of the unburned piece of wood that was dark like the cave in the hillside behind him, he could see the lit wisps of embers moving. These were the children running towards him when they saw the pig being carried back home.

It was only when he heard the roar of the bear that was next day to kill him that the man in the deer pelt lifted his eyes to the horizon and thought again as he often did, of the girl.

He had seen the girl a long time before, the day his

133

group had met the other group on the edge of the small valley in the place where the sun rose. He remembered the day well because of the girl and because there had been no fighting and there often was fighting when one group stumbled into the territory of another group and was seen.

He had noticed the girl straight away, even as both sides were showing they were peaceful and were offering the other no threat. His eyes had met her eyes and she had smiled. Her smile had dazzled and warmed him. It had been like the sun coming out.

Later, the two of them sat together by the little stream where the speckled fish splashed and rolled and tried to catch the big flies with the tall wings that kept coming out of the water and flying under the leaves. He had given her the perfectly round stone he had found in the water and she had studied it closely in her hand. She had smiled again, the same smile, the smile that had been like the sun coming out. She still had the stone clutched in her hand when his group moved on.

The night before he died, the night before the bear killed him and long after the girl had been killed by the jealousy behind the swung club, the man in the deer pelt had spent a long time looking into the fire. After he died, he had spent a long time undisturbed where they laid him.

It was not until the Kazuki Earthshifter 12000 came that his peace was disturbed and its weight and vibrations made his closed world shudder. Then the top of its great, toothed jaws reached over him and the bottom of its great, toothed jaws reached under him and gathered him up, first his femur and then his pelvis and then what remained of his half-gnawed spine.

The remains of his skull, as grey as a flint ball, were lifted with the next bite and joined the half-ton of soil and stones and chalk and the pieces of old wood and the roots and the tufts of grass and the clover and the meadow buttercup and the half-oyster shell that had somehow got there and the thirty-seven snail shells and the bit of the sheep's shoulder blade and the adder that had been basking amid the luxury of it all.

Even as he was being dropped into the back of a lorry that looked like a gigantic skip on wheels, the power was being tested in the new Cogent Electronics building and the Top Oil complex was having the control panel installed and the long, low building to be occupied by Ethical Pharmaceuticals was being painted as white as a doctor's coat.

Beyond them the refrigerator factory was starting production and the flat-pack furniture company was making its first shipment and Sumi Cameras were showing the Mayor of Farley and his group the recently completed assembly line.

Even as the man in the deer pelt was being automatically vibrated and jostled in the back of the lorry so that he could be settled deeper into it and make more room, the new cranes and storage facilities were being assembled on Farley Docks.

As the man in the deer pelt was being driven away through the haze and dust and the blue smoke of engines, the man in the suit who had been made redundant by Hamptons, the one who had been so worried because his young wife was pregnant, was being offered work on the development at the first time of asking and feeling his own clouds lighten.

Year 3, September

The law of continuing had drawn up the plan for the Baetis flies as carefully as it had drawn up the plans for everything else. Though it had decreed that Baetis flies should look quite like mayflies and should even be able to make their hazed wings become clear when they were ready to mate in the same way that mayflies could make their own wings clear when they were ready for mating, the law of continuing had written in some differences. One difference was that Baetis flies should be far smaller than mayflies, even to the extent that three Baetis flies could stand side by side on the old man's little-finger nail while one mayfly would not have looked small even in the palm of the old man's hand. Another difference was in the way the two flies would be required to lay their eggs. The law of continuing had written that Baetis flies should lay their eggs deep under water and not on the surface where the mayflies laid theirs. It had given the Baetis flies a way of doing it that made the old man marvel.

Each fly had been instructed that when she was ready to lay her eggs she should seek out something sticking up from the water and walk down it. Each fly had been told that when she had walked so far down whatever it was she had chosen and was almost touching the water, the law of continuing would move upon her and touch her. The moment the touch came to a fly, that fly would feel a tension. Then the law of continuing would press her high wings down and fold them along her back so that a bubble of air could be trapped between her wings and her body as if held in a cellophane sleeve. She would be able to haul this air deep into the water and it would be adequate for her needs as long as she stayed beneath the surface.

That was why, on the day the last of the tree-climbers were being brought out from the Hangers, the stems of the rushes and the roots of the alders and the pieces of planking that had fallen into the water from the wooden hut and the supports of the bridges and the three posts that reached up from the stream bed opposite the swans' nest all had Baetis flies walking down them, looking for places to lay their eggs.

The Baetis fly that hatched near the top of the island and that had received the same message as all the others, was fortunate to live long enough to lay. She had nearly drowned when she hatched and one of her wings stuck to the surface. She had just managed to cling to

the feather that was drifting by and to haul herself
aboard.

The feather had drifted a little way past the mouth of
the Oak Stream when it was swept close to the bank and
in under the long grasses that trailed over the water. The
fly on the feather drifted a long way through the vaulted
tunnel that the arching grasses made, while the sun
flickered and stabbed through them and her wet wings
dried.

The fly was carried along the bank that reared beside
her high as a cliff. She was carried past the place where
the first vole was nibbling the bright green shoot and
past the place where the mink had found the second
vole and left the blood on the stone and past the place
where the duck and the drake were edging softly
upstream and speaking in low syllables.

The Baetis fly survived the shoot and slide at the
edge of the falls and escaped the attentions of the
swallows carving spaces in the air. She was not seen
when the feather drifted as delicately as a mayfly
around the high bank where the martins nested. She
was seen but not injured when the water shrew scrambling above her sent an avalanche of dried earth
crashing all about.

The little fish lying far out towards the middle where
the water was deeper saw the feather but not the fly and
the trout with the scar saw the fly but not the feather.
The swans that cloned themselves in the calm water
behind the fallen willow and the grass snake that was
swimming thinly through the reflections of clouds
there, were not interested.

By the time the feather was passing the first of the three posts that reached into the air as dry and grey as old bones, the Baetis fly was opening and testing her wings. At the second of the posts opposite the swans' nest she made an attempt to fly. Near the third post she found an accommodation with the air and lifted and flew downstream to Bottom Bend.

She settled on the ash tree there. The Baetis fly clung to the underside of the leaf that already had two other Baetis flies hiding on it and, when it was time, moulted for the last time and made her wings clear as the plan required. Then she flew up among the males and was taken.

The sun was still touching the water when she flew back to the wooden posts and began to walk down the first one she reached.

The surface of the stream lay like an upturned sky before her and the light winking up at her seemed to beckon and draw. The Baetis fly did not see the deadness of the wood under her feet or the dryness of the spiked moss forest sticking up all around her. She did not see the lifelessness of the eggs that had once been below water but that now lay in the crevices, wrinkled and dry. She could not hear beyond the drowned music of the water or see beyond the washes of light that filled her with purpose. She knew nothing of the other flies that were walking down all around her, or of the way so many feet groped and traced the way her own feet groped and traced, or of all the other legs straining the way her legs were straining or of the light reflecting from every other tilting wing the way it reflected from her own.

When she was only a little above the water's surface, no further than the length of her own body from it, the Baetis fly that had almost drowned when she hatched prepared to enter the water again. The odours of the stream overwhelmed her and the halls of drowned music sang. As the light winked and tilted and lit her sides and highlighted the delicacy of her legs and reached up even to the tips of her two drawn tails, a long beam caught her eyes and held them. Then the law of continuing that been with her every instant, breathed on her and blessed her and gave her final understanding. The touch she had awaited, arrived.

The law of continuing took the two veined wings she had held high so long and pressed them back and down. The Baetis fly felt them being pressed back and down and felt her skin being drawn tight as though pulled with levers. Then she moved forward with her bubble of air clasped tightly along her back and stepped through the surface. The drowned music fell instantly silent and the echoing halls of the stream were gone. There were only gravels and stones and places far beneath her and a low, brown hum growing louder in her head.

The Baetis fly struggled and groped her way down the post while the current rummaged about her like a heavy wind and the weight of the bubble she was carrying tried to pull her back.

At the bottom of the post the Baetis fly that had once nearly drowned at the surface gripped the stone on the stream bed she had chosen. She paused there for a moment, as though waiting for a last perfecting spasm to pass; and then she dragged the weight of the bubble

141

that wanted to lift her upwards, down towards the stone's underside. There, on the clean part scoured by the eddy at the base of the post and not on the part sheltered from the current where the chokeweed cells were beginning to lengthen and divide and abut end to end, she laid her eggs in rows side by side, abutting end to end. She laid them while the brown hum rose and rose in her head and vibrated and shook her until she was spent.

When the noise inside her faded and a cold light had come and washed all purpose away, the Baetis fly that had once before nearly drowned felt the stone she had clung to pull itself from her feet and the bubble begin to lift her and her wings begin to loosen and spread so that the trapped air was released and wobbled up. When she reached the surface and was held between the light that had beckoned her so long as a nymph and the halls of drowned music now silent below, the Baetis fly that had once before nearly drowned turned inert in the water with her clear wings outstretched. A little downstream she was caught in the vortex that a stone there created.

And then the fly that had enjoyed so little use of her wings soared around and around with her wings outstretched, planing ever more steeply over as the vortex coiled around her and drank her down.

Even before the young salmon could sip her in as she passed the shingle banks, the cells of chokeweed on the other side of the stone on which she had laid her eggs in rows side by side and abutted end to end, were dividing side by side and abutting end to end as if to mimic her efforts.

Year 3, October

There had been no wind since the day it was realized that Cogent Electronics would need more water for its production line than originally thought. Even when it rained the air had been so still that the drops had fallen as straight as plumb lines and the drizzle had seeped down like weighted mist.

And so, when the first breath came and when the feather that had hung motionless so long turned slowly on its thread and lifted, it seemed an unnatural thing. The sparrowhawk was half-deceived by the movement and jinked. The spider that had been crouching by the web, started out.

The sparrowhawk had hardly brought down the robin before the next breath came. Before he had killed and half-eaten the robin the soft impressions the air made on his cheek and neck had built so smoothly and quickly into one another that the breeze might always have blown.

When the heron lifted it was as if all the heaviness so long about him, all the still weight and drag of summer, had gone. When he was near the falls the heron banked as though for the joy of it, arching his wings over the air as though gathering it all to him and began to glide. The rooks rose like black ashes from the trees on the skyline. The sedges near the swans' nest began to whisper and nod.

The wind that whipped up so quickly and blew so furiously ravaged the valley until nightfall and then dropped with a suddenness that made everything alert. The silence made prickling sounds in the ears of the rabbits under The Close and the badger dozing under Farfield opened one eye. The lights in the farm that had gone out, came on.

The moon was up and flat clouds were skimming when the wind swept back. It roared over the valley like a breaking wave. It punched holes into the woods and razed the beeches in The Close. It flattened the alders on the island and the ash trees on Longate. It ravished the old yew on Hinters and cast her aside. The row of poplars behind the farm collapsed like a fan.

By the time the wild-eyed heifers had stopped bellowing and skidding and the mares had stopped rearing and clattering in their stalls, it was almost over. The branch of the chestnut where the kestrel often perched was hanging and hinging like a broken wing. The pike was lying dead under the roots of the fallen willow where the bank that had held them, collapsed.

Before dawn had come and the wind had eased, the roof of the cow shed was rocking on its back like an upturned turtle and the door of the old stable was on the other side of the yard.

By the time the old man and his son had collapsed with fatigue, the wind had died and a silence had fallen.

In no time, the feather that had signalled the start of it all was turning on its thread again as though nothing had happened and the soft airs that touched it might have been innocent and bemused.

Year 3, November

It did not take long once the young man who had run all night amid the flying roofs and falling branches and who had managed to drag all the animals to safety, had walked the land and seen the great trees toppled like mushrooms with their roots exposed.

It did not take long after the young man and the old man who tried to help him had sat again at the table strewn with papers and the young man had said the storm had done them a favour in felling the trees and that the land was drained dry beyond remembering anyway.

It did not take long after the young man had raised his voice and said that he knew full well the land was ancient and unspoiled and had been in the family a long time but that it would also be taken by the bank unless the old man faced reality and had it permanently drained and prepared in the new way and unless the new crops were planted right now.

It seemed scarcely a moment after the old man had dozed in his chair and woken again to sit thinking of the young man's finger tracing the boundaries of the small fields that he said needed clearing and the ditches that he said needed digging deeper and the places where he said the drainage pipes would have to be laid.

It seemed but a blink after the old man had agreed in principle but said it was too late to start this year and the young man had said it was now or never and that a company he had been talking to could begin work straight away.

It seemed no time before the wind that had made the decision so bitterly disputed, seem no decision at all.

Year 3, December

The gulls and the crows had a high time while the trees that had been blown down were being cut up and dragged in chains to the fires and the remaining trees were felled so that scarcely an alder or a willow or a beech or an oak or an ash stood in any of the fields or on the banks of the stream.

The gulls and crows and magpies and rats had a high time while the oak where the barn owl had reared her broods was being dismembered and while the meadow where she had hawked in the dusk and taken voles and mice with a suddenness that was like a leaden pillow falling was being crossed with ditches and drained with pipes.

The ridge along Five Acre where the bank voles had nested and where the badgers from Farfield used to gambol, was soon levelled. The elder bush where the mayfly had rested in the mellow fastness until the law of continuing had lifted her towards heaven on the beam of light, was dragged out in no time.

The rushed bank where the warblers used to give their springs to the cuckoos was razed so easily that the machines did not notice and the roots of the ash tree where the Baetis fly had rested, resisted hardly at all.

The ground where the lapwing had wheeled year after year and where her eggs were always laid in the exact same spot, proved no problem. Nor did the tussocked place that the cock pheasants had used for their strutting and fighting and where the feathers they shed lay like bird-shavings in the grass.

The bulldozer had no difficulty upending the mole that drowned in the flood. The same high blade shattered the perfectly round stone that the man in the deer pelt had given to the girl whose smile had been like the sun coming out. The same blade an instant afterwards dishevelled the fingers that had held the stone so close and scattered the little still left of her as anonymously as grey flints.

A house-high wheel crushed the shells of the eggs that the skylark had picked up one by one and had carried far away from her nest so that the white reflecting from the insides would not gleam and attract danger.

A saw-toothed bucket pulled a tide of earth over the place where the cinnabar moth often settled and over the nettlebed where the red admirals had meandered on their pathways through the air and the same bucket mangled the brambles where the harvest mouse once feasted. The low rise where the shrew had dragged her pink, blind young one by one to safety in the flood, might not have existed.

The land was worked from dawn until dark so that no irregularity in it and no useless thing that lived on it should be missed. The kingcup roots were sliced and the yellow flag roots were shredded and the roots of the purple loosestrife were crushed to a pulp. Even the eyebright that the dock plant had been hiding above Top Bend and the ragged robin that had grown at Middle Bend and the large bed of primroses near the bridge on Longate were ploughed in.

By the time the weather had become cold and dull again and the chokeweed was dying back as it always did when the cold weather came, Barrows and Oak Meadow and Picket Close had been pushed together. By the time the dead chokeweed was lying in the margins brown and stinking and the cock salmon near the falls was feeling the pressure of his milt but could find no mate to relieve him of it, the boundaries between Farfield and Five Acre and Homefield had been removed and most of the ground there had been prepared in the new way and sown.

By the time the cock salmon near the falls had given up waiting for a mate and had swum back down the stream again to the river, Cress and East Street and Longate were joined and Hinters and Penny Furlong and Aftdown were united and The Close and Upper Down were one.

And so all the green fields that had once lain to the east of the stream and to the west, except for the section of Foremeadow that had been fenced off for the mares, were levelled and drained and treated and combed and made to look from the air like pegged-out skins. The fine lines that the tractors had cut through them were perfectly straight and perfectly spaced and the drills that had been prepared were precisely the right depth. The new seeds had been sown at regular intervals in them and all the prescribed fertilizers and pesticides were at work.

The young man who had finally made the old man see sense and who was confident now of making money by moving forward instead of losing it by clinging to the past, walked the land often to see what was being accomplished. He no longer seemed to be in such deep thought when he walked, or constantly to be throwing a chosen stone from one hand into the other and he took many photographs so that some day he could show them to the children that he and his fiancée were planning to have.

The old man who made himself busy about the farm knew in his heart that the decision had been inevitable, though he only looked at the photographs when the young man pressed him and he often felt a weariness roll over him like a wave.

Year 4, January

She had never spawned at the falls before. Each time she had spawned before it had been in the Tussock Stream because that was where the law of continuing had told her to spawn.

A few trout had swum up the Tussock Stream to spawn since before the counting of the years had begun. The elk with the tic in his brain, the one that was on his way to drown in the swamp, had terrified the fish in the Tussock Stream the day he blundered in among them. The man in the deer pelt and the girl whose smile had been like the sun coming out had watched the newly-hatched fry flashing in the Tussock Stream on the day he gave her the perfectly round stone. Claudius Nepos had often used his broadsword to skewer fish in the Tussock Stream because he liked their eggs so much. Henry de Montfort's feckless dog would chase the fish in the Tussock Stream every chance it got. It was while he was watching a hen fish dig her scoop in the Tussock Stream that the old man's father had noticed the stone axe that was now in Farley museum. There had never been a year when the trout had not spawned there.

The hen fish that the trout with the scar claimed close to the falls had spawned in the Tussock Stream twice before. The first time had been on the day that the shares in Plantains and Greenmount had begun to soar because of the contracts the two firms had won on the development. That first time, the water in the Tussock Stream had been as clear and cool as when the law of continuing first made the stream. Springs had even welled up through the bed of the Tussock Stream that year to wash her eggs from beneath while the current kept them clean on top. The hen fish had managed to spawn in the Tussock Stream the following year as well, not long after the Ministry issued another caution that the Broadchalk and the Clearwater were to be protected absolutely and the search for piped water was moved further away to make sure they were. That year, though, the hen fish had to choose a place much nearer the mouth of the Tussock Stream because higher up silt had settled in the margins and rushes and cress had grown out to secure it.

It was on the same day that the young man received the letter asking him to go to the bank for a review of progress that the hen trout learned she would not be able to spawn in the Tussock Stream a third year. Though the hen trout looked high and low for the gravels she needed if she were to spawn, she could not look high enough because all the gravel had been grubbed up from the stream bed and tipped out onto the banks as part of the drainage plan.

On the same day that the young man went to the bank to give his report on progress and house prices in Old Stinston reached an all-time high because most executives working on the development wanted a character house in a village and not one of the new ones that were being built on estates, there were many trout on the gravels downstream from the falls. They were all jostling in the centre of the stream because so many good spawning places towards the bank had been lost to silt and dead chokeweed.

The trout with the scar saw the hen fish from the Tussock Stream as soon as she neared the falls and he stayed with her as though her own shadow. The hen fish quartered the gravels near the falls looking for somewhere to spawn, but everywhere she went and the trout with the scar followed fish were already rolling and splashing and digging in the best places.

It was only on the day when the new borehole for Cogent Electronics was allowed against technical advice and one of the geologists said there were now so many holes in that area he imagined you could tear the place off like a postage stamp, that the hen fish from the Tussock Stream found a good spot to spawn. She moved onto the low mound where the gravel was as clean as gravel could be the moment the fish already on it had moved away.

The hen fish rolled onto her side there and began to dig up the same gravel the other fish had just dug up.

When she rolled and twisted and the clean stones lifted, the eggs that had just been laid under them by the other fish were exposed and carried downstream on the current.

The splashes the hen fish made flew so high into the air that Sid Hughes stopped his tractor to see what was happening. He crept low behind the hawthorn bush that for some reason had not been pulled out when the other bushes had been pulled out and crouched down.

Hughes watched the fish for a long time. He saw them dashing about and rolling onto their sides and making a commotion and sometimes he saw stones being buoyed and lifted and carried downstream as though weightless, but he could not see the eggs laid by earlier fish being lifted and exposed and carried downstream as well. He could not see the little fish that had the hollow flanks and the great hungers inside them darting out from behind their stones to eat the drifting eggs and did not know why the trout waiting to spawn kept ranging from side to side and opening their mouths or why the dabchick kept diving so often or why the duck kept up-ending and dabbling about.

Though he spent a long time with his eyes fixed on the fish, Sid Hughes never once glimpsed the light that fined to a bright point inside the head of the trout with the scar, nor did he once catch the high note that sang and sang while the hen fish from the Tussock Stream laid her eggs and the milt from the cock fish flowed. He was at completely the wrong angle to see how thin the two fish were.

155

Hughes was on the other side of the wide, brown field when the next two trout moved up onto the low mound where the gravel was as clean as gravel could be because it had been dug up so many times. He did not see the hen fish in that pair gradually dig her own scoop in it; nor did he see how fish after fish continued to move onto the same low mounds everywhere because there were so few places left that were suitable for spawning. He did not see how the eggs that had been so perfectly hidden by one pair of fish were each time dug up and exposed by the next. He did not see how the eggs that were not eaten by the fish and the birds were carried into the silted margins and onto the dead chokeweed to die.

Sid Hughes was so fascinated by the behaviour of the fish that morning that he told his mates about them at lunch time and watched them again that afternoon before fastening the chain and dragging out the hawthorn that had somehow been missed. He was on the other side of the stream and clearing out one of the ditches when the last of the trout spawned and only their eggs and a few others remained hidden and undisturbed.

By the time Peter Althorpe was spending most of his time on the Lincoln issue and Simon Goode, the biologist, was preparing for a stint as a witness at the Dorchester inquiry, the fine silt was settling again over the gravels the fish had cleaned. It was settling over the gravels and the eggs beneath them even though the trout had spawned where they had been told to spawn. It was settling over the gravels and casting shadows over the eggs even though this was the same place where there had been no small thing, not even the uttermost small detail, that the plan had not made perfect for spawning. It was settling over the gravels and casting shadows over the eggs and putting out their lights one by one.

Year 4, February

It was only days after the supermarket chain offered the young man the possibility of a contract that the stone that had been in place without moving since the fields were first sown, tilted a little to one side.

Just after Jo Hamilton and her team sat down to devise something new to attract the media because the torchlight vigil had proved a bit of a flop, the stone tilted so far over that it was scarcely this side of imbalance.

At the exact moment the third helicopter of the week was touching down at the Cogent Electronics site because of the pace things were moving, the stone that had reached the point of imbalance and that had wobbled uncertainly for what seemed an age, tumbled and rolled and crashed into the valley beneath it and earth slid down behind it like loosened shale.

When the low sun came out it lit the top of the stone lying deep in the furrow and the tip of the green shoot that had pushed it aside.

Not long after the road that had been carved into the Frontage and the Hangers was finished, the young man on the farm looked across the flat, combed land and saw the green haze of shoots growing everywhere over it and called the old man to come and look.

Year 4, March

The trout that had once owned the fine place between the island and the Oak Stream but that had afterwards been driven away from that place and many other places because he became old and weak, had given up and buried his head in the weeds a long time ago. He had died around the time the supermarket chain said it might offer the young man a contract but only if his produce was perfect in every detail and if he could deliver what it wanted in bulk.

The two thin fish that had tried to hold their places in the queue behind the trout with the scar both died because no fish anywhere else would let them in after the trout with the scar had driven them away.

The trout that had gradually been sickening like so many of them, the one that had only been able to hold the shallow lie near the Otter Stone where the dead chokeweed put a catch in his gills, died just as the new tractor was leaving the yard.

Even the trout with the scar was thinner than he should have been by the time the kingcups would have been opening if there had been any. Though he had driven away the two thin fish that lived in the queue behind him because he needed their spaces, he could not get enough food. He had an emptiness inside him because of the way the water level had fallen and because so many places that should have been making nymphs and grubs and water caterpillars and flies to feed him had been lost to the silt and to the slow-water plants that were beginning to grow again and to the chokeweed that had died and covered the margins with a kind of brown fungus and to the places around the fungus where only the sliders and the soft-bodied things could live.

The hollow that had been growing in his flanks even before the law of continuing had wrung him out on the gravels, was putting an ache all through him. There was an ache in the guts of all the fish, even inside the fish at the head of the queue behind the fallen willow.

And so, when the tractor left the yard and began to spray the fresh, green shoots with more fertilizers to help them grow and with more insecticides to kill any grubs and beetles that remained in the soil so that the produce could be as perfect as the supermarket chain wanted and its customers now demanded, there were fewer of the older fish in the stream to be disturbed by the vibrations it made and there were fewer young fish because so many eggs had died in the gravels.

When the tractor worked along the edge of the stream and the automatic sprayer sprayed everywhere behind it, the trout that had gradually been sickening like so many of them, the one that had only been able to hold the shallow lie near the Otter Stone where the dead chokeweed put a catch in his gills, was quite unmoved. He was unmoved even when Sid Hughes misjudged the turn and the sprayed granules spattered the surface like hailstones above him. He could not have been less interested when the bank collapsed and covered him.

By the time the lapwing had wheeled and turned and searched for the place where she had laid her eggs year after year but could not find it, the fertilizer that had been in the soil where the bank collapsed was beginning to leach out and the slow-water plants inhaled it as though in delirium. The nuclei in the cells of chokeweed drew it in and rejoiced and sent out more instructions, so that more cells were made into two by the membranes that crept across them and more spores burst out from the thin walls that ruptured.

By the time the cuckoo had quartered the wide, flat fields to find a home for her eggs but could not, the insecticides that had been in the soil where the bank collapsed were dissolving near the shrimp and the shrimp was feeling the stinging start.

The nymph of the grey-winged fly near the mouth of the Barn Stream felt the same kind of stinging after some granules were accidentally sprayed all around her and so did the nymph clinging to the cracked stone between the Oak Stream and the Barn Stream and so did the water caterpillars holding onto the crowfoot plant opposite what had once been Barrows.

The two furnace-eyed grubs that had begun to fight over the shrimp's body when it settled in the dip beside them stopped fighting one another when their own stinging began. When the stinging rose until it was like a fire raging within them, first the smaller grub lay on its side and then the larger; and the two of them lay side by side near the shrimp ignoring it completely; and they fought and scrabbled with their legs at nothing in the water above them and they bit and clawed at nothing in the water near their heads.

By the time all the land had been sprayed and the uniform shoots were standing straight and strong in their long, neat drills without a blemish or an egg or a living thing upon them, the two grubs and the shrimp were rocking in harmony in the deep dip together, lilting in the current that turned there.

Year 4, April

The time when the changes in the young salmon should have been completed, so that the fish were ready to move downstream to the sea after their time in the stream, had been written into the fish when their lights were switched on.

The time was the same time that had been written into young salmon since before the counting of the years had begun. It was the time when the kingcups would have been gleaming in the rich, damp fields and when the fallow deer does would have been feeling their young beginning to stir inside them.

It was the time when the springs would have been in full flow because the rains would have filled up the hills again, the time when the temperature of the water would not have become too high for the changes in young salmon to be completed. It was that time when the day was the special length that made young salmon want to head for the sea once the changes within them were done.

The message that said young salmon could go to sea when the changes in them were completed and when everything else was right but not before and not after, had been written into every young salmon that had ever swum in the stream.

By the time the trout had begun to spawn and dig up one another's eggs, the message written into the young salmon had already changed the shapes that had fitted them to the stream and shaped them the way salmon in the sea should be. By the time the first green shoot had unfurled on top of the ploughed ridge and sent the stone crashing into the valley below and sent all the earth tumbling after it like loosened shale, the message written into the young salmon had caused the spots and smudges on their sides to fade and was sending a silver pigment across their skins.

But by the time the flowers on the water crowfoot should have been starting to open and the skylark should have been spilling out his song, the springs had not risen even though for the first time in years it had rained in winter as it used to rain.

By the time the bee that was not there would have been exploring the kingcup flower that was not there and the sedge warbler that was not there would have been cocking her head to the tapping from inside the cuckoo's egg that was absent, the springs were low and the stream was already close to summer heat.

And so while the work raced ahead in the Broadchalk valley and the sun burned strongly for all the rain there had been and David Hoffmeyer was considering an extension to his site that would make it so big it would use enough electricty and water for a city of 12,000 people and by the way that was US citizens and not Brits, the message that had been written into all the young salmon was being rewritten by an older message, rarely used. The older message that was rarely used said the springs were not the right height for any salmon to go to sea and that the changes that needed to be completed could not be completed in time because the water was already too warm and it could only get warmer because summer was coming.

The colours on the sides of the young salmon began to darken again and the silver that had begun to migrate over their skins began to fade. The spots and smudges came back again, so that the young fish were camouflaged for life in the stream again and not for life in the sea.

It was on the day that the young men in masks were freeing the mink from her cage as an act of kindness, that it happened. The young salmon in the pool close to the falls, the one that had made a space for himself between the large stone that had the empty snail shell on its near side and the medium-sized stone that had the threads of chokeweed clinging to its far side, seemed to lunge at his neighbour suddenly for no reason. Then all the young salmon began to whirl and jostle with one another because the only time when everything could be right for them to go to the sea had come and gone without everything being right and the ancient message rarely used was preparing them to spend another year in the stream and the threat and the stress of it was bearing upon them.

Year 4, May

It was not that the wind was blowing more strongly than it sometimes did at mayfly time, though there were several days when the crows did more walking than flying and when the dust from the margins of the great, wide fields was spiralled into the air like genies.

It was not even that it was any hotter or colder than it sometimes was at mayfly time, though the sky was a seamless blue by day and clear and crisp at night. It was because there were no trees or hedgerows to slow it that the wind blew unfettered where the mayflies flew and created the problems. It was because the willows and the ash trees and the elder bushes and the alders and the hawthorns and the beeches and the oaks had gone that the mayflies could find no leaves to roost under so that they could be protected from the sun by day and no high branches to lift them clear of the frosts by night.

The nearest place any of the hatched mayflies could find to roost was in the steep, wooded slopes that faced in all around and that was where the mayfly from the island was blown: across the one great field where Hinters and Penny Furlong and Aftdown had been, to the beech tree on the edge of the wood.

Her wings were strong, but only as strong as the law of continuing had written in the plan. They were strong enough to beat back the gravity that wanted to drag her down, but only for as long as it would have taken her to reach the bushes and the trees that had lined the banks and the ditches and that all the generations before her had used. They were strong enough, once she had found a leaf to hide under high above the ground and had changed her skin for the last time, to carry her among the males that would have been rising and falling in columns behind the hedges and trees that all the generations of males before had used. They were strong enough to carry her back to the stream again when she was ripe with eggs, but only from those places close by where all the generations before her had hidden and mated and then only if there was some shelter from the wind if shelter were needed. The wings she had been given were strong, but only this strong.

And so when the mayfly lifted in the shelter of the alder that still stood on the island and misjudged the airs, the wind grabbed her and drowned her and carried her away.

The wind carried her over the places where the hawthorn had spread its lace and where the dog-rose had wound and where the barn owl had sometimes rested on the post. It carried her past the place where the single oak had once stood and where the saw had whined and where the branches had snapped and crackled in the flames. The wind carried her over the wide, flat fields that were winking with the wings of the flies that the wind had cast down. It blew her over the regiments of green shoots that stood on the parched, brown earth to the beech tree. It was only there, in a space safe in the branches but far from the stream, that the mayfly found a leaf to cling to and clung.

The mayfly from the island held her wings shut tight and waited as the sun went down and the bats came out and the moon honed its sickle on the thin winds all about it. All the flies under all the leaves about her folded their wings tightly and waited while the stream gleamed like tinsel on the far horizon and frost crusted the flies that had fallen in the open.

It was long after the hollow cough of the pheasant had prompted the blackbird to sing and the day's chorus had begun; long after the cardboard flap of the wood pigeon's wings had caused the sparrowhawk to look up and tilt down; long after the swifts and finches had headed out to the stream to feed on mayflies again that the law of continuing passed over the mayfly from the island and prepared her for mating the way mayflies had been prepared since before the counting of the years had begun.

It was long after the hot sun had warmed the ground again and thawed the bodies of the mayflies that had either not been able to reach the woods on their way from the stream or else had not been able to reach the stream on their way back from the woods, that the mayfly stopped opening and testing her wings.

It was only when Earl Johnson, the Director of the Cogent Electronics site, was being told a blackbird's nest had been found in the powerhouse and was agreeing to reschedule some work there so that it need not be disturbed, that the mayfly from the island joined the males and was mated. It was only when the fullness of her body urged her and the odours of the stream inhaled and consumed her that she left the cover and the shade.

The wind was strong, but she had still gone a long way over the wide, flat fields by keeping low and out of the worst of it before a gust unhinged her and threw her down.

The mayfly with the broken wing lay for a long time between the shoots that stood high and straight all about her, at first unable to move. Then she managed to struggle upright and she swayed as though dazed beside the male whose wings had subsided when the night frost reached through him so that now he lay crucified, embracing the warm earth. She lurched unsteadily beneath the fly that the sun had dehydrated and that spun slowly as a clock wheel from a spider's thread. The mayfly from the island knew only the uselessness of wings and the menace of the sun and the need to reach the shade that the high shoots offered.

A little way above the ground, on the first shoot she reached, she stopped. She clung to the shoot for a long time, one wing held high and sparkling above her and the other hanging downwards, awkwardly awry. All afternoon she kept edging sideways, keeping the stem between herself and the sun. All afternoon the sun angled and stalked her.

About the time that the last nymphs of the day were leaving their cool, dark tunnels in the bed of the stream and were launching themselves upwards to meet the needs of the birds, the mayfly from the island could find no strength to move again and clung where she was, drained and spent. The high sun swung and found her. It warmed her upright wing first and then the wing hanging downwards awkwardly awry and then her back and sides.

By the time the last birds were back in their roosts and sleeping, the fields were glistening as though with dew. All across the wide, flat fields where the green tussocks had grown and where the blossom and flowers had scented the air, all along the ditches where the hedgerows and trees had given their shelter to the flies and where generations of mayflies had been able to fly where they needed to fly, the moon lit the mayflies that had been cast down and sparkled from their wings when they trembled in the frost.

Before the hatching of the mayflies was over, even before the supermarket buyer had come to inspect the farm again and the fledglings had safely flown from the powerhouse at Cogent Electronics, the young man was installing pipes to take water from the stream. The pipes were shooting the water in wide, arched curtains across what once had been Cress and Homefield onto the tall, green shoots that grew there.

Before the last of the mayflies was gone and the rare flower found on the Top Oil site had been gently lifted and moved to a safe place but not before the *Stinston Herald* had been called to photograph it being gently lifted and moved, the body of the mayfly from the island was crinkled and brittle in the open drill and her eggs were as lifeless as the dust.

Year 4, June

'What's the matter, love?' Jim Hamilton could tell the moment the front door closed and her footsteps were in the hall that she was uptight about something.

'Have you seen the *Herald*?' Jo Hamilton tossed the paper onto the settee beside him and made straight for the rocking chair – her comfort chair, he called it. 'Letters, page 13. Someone made redundant by Hamptons last week, got a job with Cogent this week. More pay, big-company benefits, the lot.'

'Lucky old him. So what?'

'He's going on about environmentalists in general, SAVE in particular and me specifically. He says we're tree-huggers, trying to stop the clock. Go on, read it. Top right-hand corner.' She spotted the Scotch and water on the table at his side. 'I need one of those.' She groaned, hauled herself back to her feet and went to the cabinet. He read while she poured.

Before he was half-way through he was nodding and half-smiling to himself. 'But come on, love. You've seen this stuff a hundred times during the last couple of years. There's nothing new here. There's—'

'Just makes me despair, that's all. If you actually stand up for anything these days, people assume you're some kind of fanatic. Especially if it's something to do with the environment. It's part of industry's strategy to make you look like that. The Government's, too. They try to make you look unreasonable or unbalanced. If you get in their way, they try to neuter you in the public mind.'

Her husband searched for truth in the depths of his glass. 'Well, hang on. This chap's writing personally, not for the company. Anyway, some companies are pretty responsible. Lots of environmental projects are sponsored by business.'

She was back in the chair now, rocking herself gently. 'Only when they see a benefit to themselves. Only when they want to soften their image in general or to distract from something specific that could give them a problem. At the end of the day it's only another invest-ment to be turned on and off. It's always maximum profits first, environment second.'

Jim Hamilton opened the paper and looked at the letter again. 'I really do think he's just talking priorities, love. You can understand it. He'd have been on the dole if it hadn't been for Cogent. What's it he says . . . ?' Hamilton flexed the paper to make it easier to read. 'He says, "You don't have to be a tree-hugger to worry about the future. Lots of people worry. But the truth is the earth's not only full of woods and settlements and badgers and bats, it's full of human beings. At the end of the day, we have to survive as well." What's the matter with that? Common sense, isn't it?'

Hamilton knew he was sailing close to the wind, reading it out like that. It was old, old ground for both of them. They always ended up counting exactly the same angels on exactly the same pinheads. Sometimes, though, he felt he had to push her a bit. It helped to clear a build-up of unspoken frustrations, for both of them. It helped to clear the air.

She shook her head. There he was, same old patronizing, myopic view. 'But that's exactly what I'm talking about, surviving. If we go on like this we're going to end up digging ourselves and polluting ourselves off the face of the earth. If we don't blow ourselves off it or genetically modify ourselves off it first.'

He smiled. 'Not your best piece of self-expression, love.'

She ignored him. 'The earth doesn't need us, any more than it needed dinosaurs. There's nothing written that man is here for ever. In the fullness of time we'll be just one more extinct species come and gone. The big difference is, we'll be the first species to make ourselves extinct. We'll self-destruct. We've already started.'

Jim Hamilton opened the packet of peanuts on the table, tipped them into one of the cut-glass bowls his mother had given them and passed it to her. She always went cosmic like this. One minute you were talking about the Frontage or bats or something, next she'd be onto the end of the world.

'Problem is,' he said, 'human beings are not standing on the sidelines, refereeing anything – we're a part of nature ourselves. We're the human animal, doing what the human animal does. Badgers dig holes, bats hang upside down, man changes things. That's the way we are. We do it because we can. We do it to improve things for ourselves.'

His wife screwed up her face. 'D'you know – I despair of you, I really do. We've got choices, haven't we? We can understand cause and effect, can't we? Try putting your argument to someone drowning on an atoll because the oceans are rising because the icecaps are melting. Try telling them it's all perfectly natural – it's just the rest of us changing and improving a few things so we can have more cars and freezers.' She waved at the window. 'It's obvious we have to start saying no – and not just to things in our own back yard. Every new generation means millions more to feed and more needs to be met. We're on a mad helter-skelter. Common sense says we can't go on as we are. That's what this chap in the *Herald* doesn't have, common sense. Or you!'

He shrugged. 'Oh, come on. There are no villains in this, Jo. There are just folks like you and me, trying to rub along. The problem with you is . . .' He stopped in mid-sentence and shrugged. Beethoven's Fifth was drowning him out and her head was buried in a book.

Year 4, July

The otter had not visited the stream for a long time. She had marked it from time to time, laying down the scent that told other otters to keep away, but she had not explored it since the time she chased the great trout that had escaped from the farm.

The otter had visited the stream often when it held lots of fish. She had taken three of the pike that had lived under the trees and that had lain like logs on the bottom and she had enjoyed many of the young trout and salmon that had leapt and splashed in the pool below the falls. Twice at night she had found salmon with the smell of the sea on them, great fish that had surged and leapt and made great waves when she chased them and that had thrashed and thrown pieces of moon into the air when she caught them, while the round-eyed voles had peered from their entrances and the ducks had made a commotion and turned in tight circles and while the swans and their young had lurched into the water and melted into the night like mist.

Many times when the otter had killed a fish, she had towed it to the big stone near the Cattle Drink to eat it. Then the fish farm had been made on the bend of the Clearwater and from time to time the farmed trout had escaped. Sometimes the fish slipped through the grilles that allowed the clean water from upstream of the farm to flow into the ponds where they were kept. Sometimes they slipped through the grilles that fed water laden with excrement back into the river once the trout had used it. Many thousands of fish had escaped when the Clearwater flooded at the same time as the stream flooded and thousands more had been freed when the chestnut tree came down in the gale and ripped one of the grilles clean out.

The otter had enjoyed the easy pickings that resulted. The farmed fish had no experience of living in the wild and they often settled in places that made them easy to see and sometimes, even if they had been in a place a long time, they failed to change their colouring so that they blended better into the background to make themselves more difficult to detect. Many other tricks that the wild trout had learned to help keep themselves alive had been bred out of the farmed trout to make them bigger and easier to control and all of this had made things easier for the otter, as well.

It was because the farmed fish had been so easy to catch that the otter had stayed near the farm so long.

Then the fish had gradually got fewer. Then the taste of the new escapees had changed because the formula of the food they were fed was altered to make them grow more efficiently and to help them become more resistant to the diseases that kept breaking out. Then the road traffic had increased because of the work on the development and the otter had gradually ranged wider.

The otter had smelled the change in the stream that entered the Clearwater many times before, from a distance. She had tasted the strangeness of it on the water and had hesitated many times on the bank opposite the place where the stream flowed in, standing up on her hind legs and resting on her tail, looking across at the entrance.

On the night when the single salmon leapt so far downstream that she could not see it, around the time some of the long strands of chokeweed between Top Bend and Middle Bend were breaking away under their own weight and lodging elsewhere, the otter again paused on the banks of the Clearwater opposite the stream. Again the otter sat up on her hind legs and smelled the strange smells and made small lapping noises with her tongue as though tasting a new taste and stared into the gloom with her dark, round eyes.

Far downstream, the salmon she could not see but that could also smell and taste the strangeness being carried into the Clearwater, leapt again. The salmon seemed to wait in mid-air while the moonlight drained from him drip by drip before crashing back down into a pit of foam. Then he hurled himself into the air a third time. It was almost as if the images that had lured him there were becoming distorted and making him confused, as if he were jumping to check he was where he was supposed to be, according to the plan. As though the third leap had been a signal, the otter slid into the water from the bank opposite the stream, melting upwards from her nose. A silken ripple reached up the brown ribbon behind her and reached down again. The water folded over the place she had entered and smoothed it out.

For a time it was as though there was a clumsiness about the otter when she reached the entrance to the stream. She had to turn sharply to avoid the silt that reached out under the surface like an accusing finger. Then she caught her foot on the bed of the stream where it should have been deep and stirred up clouds of black debris and wobbling bubbles. Then she had to stop twice to pull away the strands of chokeweed that trailed from her hind foot like a leaden web.

The otter followed the line of the least-slow water all the way upstream, weaving in and out of the silt beds and the chokeweed that had not been there last time she visited; staying close to the cress bed near the new concrete bridge that had been built to replace the old bridge on Longate that the old man had made in his youth. The only reason she faltered at the bridge at all was to sniff at the empty nest that the coot had left and at the broken shells around it and at the small, clawed pad marks in the dust.

It was on her way past what had been Picket Close, near one of the sections of bank that had fallen in when the bulldozer passed, that she smelled the fresh green vileness that the mink had made to mark that place as its own. She passed a dried vileness with bones and fur

181

in it opposite the post that the Baetis fly had crawled down to lay the eggs that the chokeweed had long since entombed. She saw a vileness with a coot's feather in it close to the place where the cygnets were sleeping and where the cob had his neck laid along his back with his beak under his wing and one eye open, following every movement she made.

The otter heard the chattering of the mink when she was opposite the fallen willow and then saw the mink on the stone: the stone that had once been far out into the water and that she had so often used herself, but that now was a part of the bank. The mink that had been freed from her cage by the young men in masks because it was a kindness was crouching low, gnawing at what remained of the duck. Then the otter smelled another stink on the air and saw the five young mink padding in line up the far bank close to the water, each reaching nose to each trailing tail, undulating and gleaming over the ground like a furred snake. The otter felt no fear of the mink but smelled their smell and felt the pressure of their presence and knew the deadness in the water upstream. She turned, melted into the water again and swam downstream.

At the entrance to the Clearwater she turned right and headed upstream. She was far around the bend when the salmon that had leapt three times behind her earlier in the night, slid into the pool opposite the stream entrance where the salmon always rested and rested there. She was far away and asleep in her holt when the letter was typed.

Year 4, August

The last of the young man's harvest had been collected by the supermarket chain and the first land to have been harvested had already been ploughed and sprayed again by the time Paul Tyler sent his letter to the Minister.

Tyler's management team had thought it a good idea. The whole development had been pretty contentious but it had gone as smoothly as these things do and everything was looking good. The area for miles around was beginning to feel the benefits of the jobs and money and fresh blood pouring in. There was still a way to go but the end was in sight. What better than to get the Minister, the local man who had proved so supportive to the project, to come down and officially open it, so to speak – to cut a ribbon or something, make a speech? The Minister would know what to say to get a headline. It would round the whole thing off nicely. In about a year seemed right. Things should be ship-shape in a year.

The week the letter was sent was an education for the salmon. It was not that the little salmon had not been told. The law of continuing had told every salmon that ever swam about the thing in the water. The law of continuing had whispered to the little salmon even when he was still curled up in his egg and blind that warm water was to be avoided. The law of continuing had not mentioned that warm water contained less oxygen than cool water, but it had told the little salmon there was a thing in warm water that would press on his gills if it got the chance.

The law of continuing had told the little salmon that the thing in warm water could press on his gills so hard it could make them heavy and difficult to move. It had told the little salmon that if he stayed in warm water long enough, lights would prickle his eyes. It had even said that if he ever stayed in warm water too long, the thing would press on his gills so hard that he would not be able to move them at all and then black waves would roll over the sun. All of this had been explained clearly to the little salmon that the heron accidentally dropped.

By the time Paul Tyler's letter arrived in the Minister's office, the little salmon that the heron had accidentally dropped into the chokeweed had still not been able to find a way out. Though the little salmon found himself in a clearing in the chokeweed, every avenue he explored was closed off as though by a portcullis or a tangled web. The longer he looked and the hotter the sun blazed and the more the chokeweed inhaled the fertilizers in the water, the more the cells divided and abutted end to end and the more dense the web became and the less the current was able to pass through it to keep him cool.

By the time the Minister's office had replied that the Minister would be pleased to come and officially open the development in a year's time, the young salmon that was trapped in the chokeweed seemed to be learning that all he had been told about the thing in the water was true. He began to open and close his mouth quickly and to push out with his gills very hard and then he started dashing about between the green walls that drew in about him and the green floor that lifted under him and the green ceiling that lowered as though to catch and hold him.

On the afternoon when the sun burned hotter than it had burned at any time since the otter had encountered the mink, all movement of water through the clearing stopped. Then it was as though the little salmon could feel the thing in the water pressing on his gills with an effortless power and the pricklings in his eyes begin. He seemed to summon himself up as if from outside of himself and started to drive at the chokeweed blindly.

By the time the Minister's acceptance was firmly in his diary and the last of the young man's land had been ploughed and sprayed again and the first land to have been ploughed and sprayed had already been seeded again, the little salmon's education was almost complete. Though he pressed out with his gills his gills would scarcely move out and the light from his sun was fading.

Year 4, September

The great salmon that had done all the leaping on the night the otter encountered the mink, had been waiting in the Clearwater opposite the mouth of the stream a long time. He had been far away when the law of continuing had sent the scents through the water to find him and guide him back.

He had entered the Broadchalk when the last of the mayflies were still dying in the fields where the hedgerows used to be. He had leapt the leap in Farley as the visitor was asking if many salmon still came into the Broadchalk and someone was saying yes but for some reason not as many as before.

The great salmon had entered the Clearwater around the time the young man was arranging delivery of the new, improved fertilizer; yet for all the length of his journey and for all that he had been in the Clearwater so long and had lain so long in the pool opposite the stream entrance, the taste in the water coming out of the stream still held him back.

It was not until the trees on the skyline were wrestling with the wind and the leaves were being stripped away like migrating birds that the urgency of the salmon's need overcame the reluctance that restrained him and he moved.

The salmon crossed the Clearwater like a grey shadow sidling and followed the same line up the stream that the otter had taken. He swam past the coot's nest that still lay littered with eggshells and where the marks of the mink's feet were impressed in the dust, eased up the gentle bend along what had been Picket Close, edged around the shingle banks and stopped in the pool at Bottom Bend because salmon had always stopped there and because anyway the water beyond was too shallow for him to swim in.

The salmon did not move from the pool beneath the kingfisher's nest at Bottom Bend once he arrived there. He did not move even when the surface became prickled with rain and puddles formed on the banks.

Though it rained as much as it had often rained at that time in the past, the water around the salmon did not lighten or lift because of the springs and the plan. The plan that the law of continuing had made had no pipes in it anywhere and the rain that had been sent was being sucked from the ground that fed the springs faster than it could fall. And so the salmon lay close to the stream bed, leaden and dull. The pictures he had been given to help bring him there, the images of bouncing light and clean gravels and drifting nymphs and the glimpsed outlines of mayflies flickering overhead, might have faded from the salmon's head utterly. The ache in his gut was growing and the stink of the choke-weed was putting a catch in his gills because the chokeweed was dying as it had always died when the cool weather came.

During the week when the starlings began to flock and swirl as though caught in wild currents and the Minister's office asked if the date of the official opening could be moved from the Tuesday to the Thursday, the bed of the stream suddenly reached up and touched the salmon on his belly and seemed to waken him as though from a dream. It was as if a high fright passed through him. He suddenly turned and dashed down-stream, swimming faster and faster, sending waves slopping up the banks and making the rushes shush and sway.

All the fish that saw the salmon seemed to become seized with his urgency and fright and to pass it to others. All along the stream from the entrance where the wash of the salmon carried the dark cloud out into the Clearwater to the gravels below the falls that no salmon could now reach, the trout began to whirl and dash about and leap into the air and to open their jaws and flare their gills and to jostle for one another's places.

189

Year 4, October

The mink that had sensed no danger when the otter had come but that had still waited until the otter's silhouette had melted into the skyline before rejoining her kits, had been on her own since the last of the kits had left.

She had made many dens since the young men in masks had freed her from her cage and she had found the stream, but the hole under the fallen willow was the best.

The tangled roots screened it from the front. There was only one small hole on the upstream side where the water had poured in during the flood and a larger hole at the downstream side where the water had poured out. Between the two holes and reaching deep into the bank there was the lofted space she had lined with old leaves and pieces of rush and it was in here, about the time the mayflies were hatching, that she had delivered her young.

Never once had the den been found by the men working the machines on the field overhead and never once had she been spotted entering or leaving by the men on the machines on the wide field opposite, though twice one of them had found half-eaten coots on the bank that he did not think could be the work of a fox.

The stream had been an excellent place at first. It had so many hiding places and hunting places and so much cover. The kits had thrived on all the trout she had caught by swimming and diving and on all the coots and ducks and water hens she had at first brought to them and that later they had learned to take for themselves; and because of all the moles and voles that had been there. Her kits were fluid and strong when they left. Their teeth were sharp and their coats were bright. Their noses reached for every smell that was available for reaching and their eyes let no movement go.

From time to time, the mink that had been freed from her cage by the young men in masks because it was a kindness would bestow the gift of stillness on a vole or a rabbit or a bird if one moved near because the law of continuing had given all mink that gift to bestow.

She saw the vole that would not be still on the morning the Minister's officials wrote and moved the day of the opening back from the Thursday to the Tuesday again. She saw it move soon after she awoke and went to the edge of her den. The movement was near the place where, the night before, the fox had jumped four-square on the skyline and had later trotted off with a limpness in his mouth.

The mink held onto the movement that teased the corner of her eye near the place where the alder used to be. There was a dim shape in the entrance to the hole in the bank. A strand of weed was hanging out from the hole and steadily edging into it, glistening and wet. Once she had seized the movement, it was as though the space between it and the mink's brain had the power of seduction; as though that single distraction had become the purpose of existence.

The mink slipped out from her den and moved upstream along the bank, past the places with the smells without heeding them, past the places with shadows without pausing. She smelled only vole and saw only the hole in the bank where the long wet strand was slowly being drawn upwards, catching the light. She slid into the water and swam from her own bank towards the other.

The mink left the stream with a movement so fluid it joined the water with the land. She was hurrying but not running, undulating and turning, everywhere her body following the line of the earth. It was as though the roots and the stones and the mounds and the awkward-nesses and the dips of the bank were lying down before her. It was as though there was the smell of vole every-where and the beckoning of weed everywhere; as though the whole valley was filled with the hush of the grasses parting and with her hot, caught breaths and with the clicks that her claws made when they caught the edges of stones.

The vole had made other galleries in the bank, just as

the voles before him had made galleries before the mink had come and bitten through their necks to bestow the gift of stillness. The bank beneath the old sand martins' nests was filled with passageways and chambers that generation upon generation of voles had made, though all that was in most of them now were bones and empty shells and the stench of rat.

All the passages and galleries had been lived in until the drought had come. Many of them had been lived in until the boreholes had been sunk so far away from the Broadchalk and the Clearwater that the water abstracted could not affect either of them. Then cracks had begun to pattern the walls and fine dust and small stones had sprinkled down from the roofs and the mink had arrived.

The gallery where the vole with the weed was crouching had not been made long. The vole had made it himself and he was in his usual place close to the tunnel entrance, with the shoot clasped between his feet the way a squirrel holds a nut.

The sun reflected from the water and reached in behind him, casting moving shadows through the chambers he had made. A brilliance edged the haired root that hung from the roof by his head.

The shoot of weed was as crisp as water-celery and the sounds of chewing filled the vole's head. He could hear nothing beyond them. From time to time he seemed to pause and savour a mouthful and then he would draw in more of the long, green strand and chew that.

The sun lit the wet weed hanging out from the hole. Even from a long way down the bank, far beyond the places that the soft pad and click of paws had already passed and where the hot breaths left on the air had cooled again and the parted grasses were still again, the weed glinted like an enticement beneath the entrance to the tunnel.

Each time the vole ate a little more and pulled in a little more, the glistening strand lifted. Each time it lifted it seemed that the mink that had been freed from her cage by the young men in masks because it was a kindness, was urged forward. Each time it moved it seemed to make the mink more eager to bestow the gift of stillness that was hers to bestow. Each time the strand lifted her hot breaths rasped faster and her claws clicked quicker and the silence was tightened about her to a high-wire hum.

Year 4, November

The chokeweed had stopped growing not long after the young salmon that the heron had dropped was learning there really was a thing in the water that could press on his gills and close them. By the time the weather had cooled and the morning mists had come, the chokeweed had begun to soften and decay.

It was not that the fertilizers seeping in from the fields had lost their potency and that the stream no longer contained the richness the chokeweed needed to thrive that it stopped growing. It was because the time had como when the law of continuing had instructed chokeweed everywhere to stop growing, that it stopped. The law of continuing had never allowed chokeweed to grow if the weather was cold and dull, which was why chokeweed mostly decayed in winter. The plan had always been clear that chokeweed would need sunlight and warmth before it could thrive.

And so once the short, dark days started to gather, the chokeweed that had claimed all the shallow places and that had reached out its long tentacles to explore most of the deeps, began to darken and break down and drift away.

A dead weight of chokeweed pulled up the withered roots of the water crowfoot that had long since died for want of current near the Otter Stone and sent the leeches and the flat worms and the things that lived in tubes lashing and crawling to find new places.

A dead weight of it pushed against the lank plants behind the island and pulled them away. It pushed and tumbled like dark capes over the slow-water weeds on the long, straight reaches, but mostly they lowered themselves under it and the leeches and the flatworms and the crawlers and the biters that had made their homes in the silt there were able to hang on.

All around the insides of the bends from Top Bend downstream, all along the sides of the island and the backwaters either side of the falls, all through the place where the cattle used to drink and the swans had finally left for good, the matted clumps of chokeweed tumbled and turned. They rolled mute and blind all the way below Bottom Bend to the new concrete bridge where the coot's nest lay with the blown dust and seeds and broken shells inside it and where the pad marks of the mink that had been freed as a kindness were impressed in the ground.

The matted clumps slid over the stone that had the

grub of the brown-winged caddis fly on it, close to the bank where the bear's skull lay buried and though the caddis grub gripped the stone with all the power her legs had in them, she was pulled away as though her legs had no power.

The chokeweed tumbled through the deep water not far from the place where the elk had stumbled a second time on his way to drown in the swamp and though the nymph on the stone there clung with all the power she could find and though she strained and clung until a redness must have pulsed through her head and the sinews in her legs must have burned and snapped, the stoneclinger was swept away as though her clinging meant nothing.

The chokeweed brushed away the water snail that had been moving from the grey stone to the brown stone not far from the place where the man in the deer pelt had first spoken to the girl whose smile had been like the sun coming out and it left the water snail upturned high and dry in his shell in the margins with his blind foot searching and sucking wetly on the air.

A sullen weight of chokeweed pushed against the sycamore that had fallen across the stream's mouth and became so tangled in its branches that the sycamore almost became a dam.

It was about the time that the trout near the sycamore turned around and tried to move into the Clearwater at last and found she could not, that the machines were started up again. It was just as the trout with the scar had to move aside when the fallen willow flexed under the weight of chokeweed caught in it and the silt trapped at its base lifted black as a threat, that the first machine began to work the first of the wide, flat fields again.

On the day the invitations to the opening ceremony were printed, the wind whipped up. It blew so hard that the two trees deliberately left beside the farm were reminded of its power and made to worship before it. The wind whirled the topsoil into the air like genies. It settled a film over the stream that fish could not see through and the film gritted in their gills when it sank.

The soil lay whorled in the backwaters like fallen smoke. The new, improved fertilizer that the machines had sprayed onto it added new stains to the others that were already in the water. The reeds and the sedges and the lank weeds absorbed them. The cells of chokeweed that always clung to life somewhere, inhaled them and stored them.

It was because the drought had come and the bore-holes had come that the stains in the water were so strong. It was because the drought had come and the boreholes were taking water faster than the plan was replacing it that the springs had not risen for three winters in a row and the stains in the water were so little diluted. Neither the trout with the scar nor the gaunt cock fish with the hooked jaw and the huge head nor any of the other fish could see the stains put into the water by the dead chokeweed and the insecticides and fertilizers and by the strange chemicals that seeped into the stream from the cracked pipe under the farm. The fish could not see the stains though the stains were everywhere about them and the fish could not feel the stains though they were everywhere passing through them.

In the places where the chokeweed lay dark as fungus on the stream bed because the springs had not risen to sweep it away and in the piled-high silts that covered the margins for the same reason and in the new, still places that had decaying weed and the dead eggs of the Baetis flies and the caddis flies and the lank fish in them, silver bubbles wobbled up and burst with a foul smell and the soft-bodied things rejoiced.

Year 4, December

The trout with the scar moved forward.

All the changes that the spawning time would make in him were made, all the changes that the stains in the water would begin in him were begun. There was inside him only the need to move forward that had long been written into him and a clenching in his gut and a dullness solid as a stone in his head.

The need to move towards the gravels seized all the trout that were still in the stream and that were capable of movement, though many fish that had moved towards the gravels last time were not moving this time.

The hen fish that had spawned with the trout with the scar last time was not there because she had been driven away from her lie by one of the great farmed trout that entered the stream and she had grown weak and sickened from parasites and died. It was the same for the hen fish above the shingle banks and the hen fish near the middle of the three old posts and the cock fish opposite the top post.

The old cock fish that had lived near the bank where Picket Close had been was not there because a shoal of farmed trout had settled in about him and the little fish were so many and flashed and darted so quickly that they took everything that was edible before he could reach it and he starved. It was the same for the old cock fish opposite him and the hen fish behind him and the hen fish behind that.

Though there were many fish not in the queue heading for the gravels that had been in it last time, the queue was still longer than before.

All the little farmed trout in the shoal that had taken the food meant for the wild fish moved forward, even though they did not know why they moved forward. All the big farmed trout that had driven away the wild fish from their lies moved forward though the eggs and milt inside them were lifeless.

Nearly all the wild trout were in the queue also, even the tiny cock fish that had lived near the place where the seepage from the broken pipes under the farm came in.

The stains in the water that could not be seen or felt even though they were all around him and through him, had boon working on the little cock fish since he had been in his egg. They had made changes in the little trout that the law of continuing had not planned for any trout.

The little cock fish that joined the queue heading for

the gravels no longer had the secret places inside him that a little cock fish should have inside. The secret places that should have been like the secret places in any other little cock trout had long begun to behave like the secrets hidden inside a female trout, so that the little cock fish was confused and went up to the gravels though he should have been too young to know anything about gravels and should have been going to them for a different reason, anyway.

Wherever the little cock fish swam, a stream of thin odours seeped from his vent and told the other fish near him that the little cock fish had been made partly a hen fish and some of the ripe male fish began to approach him and harass him.

Even the little hen trout that had the stains passing through her, the one that had somehow managed to survive in the desolate place near the old swans' nest moved forward, though the eggs she had inside her were wrinkled and dead.

The trout with the scar reached the gravels close to the falls the same day that David Hoffmeyer said he would be present when the Minister opened the development if he could and the heads of Top Oil and Ethical Pharmaceuticals and the flatpack furniture business and the paint laboratory and the food processing plant and the dye works and the printing works all said they would be there as well.

Many of the farmed trout that had escaped were already on the gravels and the two that were almost as big as salmon had taken the one clean place left for spawning. The cock fish kept driving all the other fish away from it, even though the great hen was sterile and though the milt inside the cock fish could have fertilized nothing and though the stones beneath them both were so cemented in by silt that they could not be dug up no matter how hard the hen fish was flailed against them.

Many wild trout were driven away from the gravels because there was no room and the escaped farm fish began to whirl and bite those around them because that was what they always did when they were jammed together and stressed.

The escaped trout had known so many stresses when they were jammed tight together in the ponds on the fish farm that it was almost as though they had been conditioned to whirl and bite. They had even been stressed and conditioned when they were fed. Every time the man who fed them had gone near the tubs where the food made from pulped wild fish was kept, the fish had thrashed and churned at the sight of it as though a switch inside each of them had somehow been thrown. Every time the man had swung his arm and thrown scoops of food so that the small pieces of ground fish and meal smattered above them, the trout in the pools thrashed and churned and competed to get them. Even when the man amused his visitors by standing on the side of the pool and waving his arm as though throwing food, the fish thrashed and churned at the sight of it though he threw them nothing. Every time the trout in the fish farm had been made agitated by experiences like these, they had swum around and around in tight circles in their ponds and leapt and splashed until the water rocked and surged up the banks around them and they bit one another on the tail.

The wild fish that dashed away from the gravels when the farmed trout started to whirl and bite hid anywhere they could, but still many of them died because they were given infections with their wounds that were nowhere in a wild fish's plan.

Year 5, January

'We only have a few minutes left. I want to bring this week's edition of *Dilemmas* to an end by asking each of our panellists to sum up what they see as the essential points.'

Lisa Pearce turned to Sir John Plumpton. 'Sir John, your family has owned the Hanger Hall estate for three hundred years. You've done well out of this personally by selling land for housing and the like. Remind us what the rest of the community has got.'

As the camera swung towards him and Sir John nodded, the hen trout that was desperate to spawn was being thrashed at the gravels again in an attempt to loosen the stones that were embedded in the silt. More scales broke away from her flank but the stones did not move. 'Well, as I say, it's the old story. Until recently, the land employed pretty well everyone. Those who didn't work on the land worked for one or another of the small, local companies. Then mechanization came and farming became an industry in its own right. Farms got bigger – yes, my own among them – and the number of jobs fell. People began to drift away. The growth of large companies elsewhere, the influx of cheap products from abroad, technology, the attractions of life and work in the city all combined to draw more young people away and put local businesses under pressure. For nearly half of my lifetime, this area has been bleeding to death.'

As he paused and the cameras showed Earl Johnson, Director of the Cogent Electronics site nodding and Jo Hamilton making a note on her pad, the pressures inside the hen fish became too great. Her vent suddenly inverted and a pink rim showed and then waters tinged with red seeped out. 'Today the picture is completely different. There is high investment in the area, there are as many jobs available as people to fill them, we have an influx of new, skilled young professionals and a level of spending that is pulling the entire region out of recession.'

'Thank you, Sir John. Earl Johnson, tell us on behalf of a major multinational, what benefits your company has seen by investing here.' Johnson nodded. The trout with the scar smelled the odours coming from his mate and moved towards her.

'I'd rather tell you what brought us here, first. Cogent Electronics could have put this facility into several countries. If we hadn't had a particular problem at our plant in Milan, Italy might have got it. It was touch-and-go whether or not we put it into Germany, so in that sense there was an element of chance in the decision to come here at all. There is an element of chance in all these things. However, we did see an opportunity here. We told your Government the kinds of things we were looking for – a level playing field for our products, among them. But we couldn't have come without every-thing else – a port equipped with the kinds of facilities we needed, good roads with access to the motorway network, the kinds of housing and local environment that would be of interest to the skilled people we needed to attract, that kind of thing. Your Government bent over backwards to make it possible. It might well have taken a greenfield site to give us all of that, I don't know. Either way, you can't make an omelette without breaking eggs.'

The trout with the scar quivered alongside the hen fish and her mouth was wrenched wide and his mouth was wrenched wide and both their dams burst and the first of her empty eggs spilled onto the flat stream bed. Pearce nodded. 'And the end results are those Sir John spelled out?'

'For the community, yes. For Cogent Electronics they were increased business volumes and profits. For the UK, in addition to the money and jobs we put directly into the economy, it meant increased exports, reduced imports and a fair degree of technological spin-off.'

Pearce glanced at the clock on the wall and swung in her chair. 'Jo Hamilton of SAVE, that sounds a pretty good package. What's your problem?'

Hamilton swallowed the sip of water she'd just taken from her glass. 'My problem is the hidden cost. We've

207

lost two historic sites and an area of outstanding natural beauty. I don't mean how the statutory bodies define historic and beautiful and what's worth preserving, I mean how ordinary people define them. Public bodies come and go with Governments and fashions. Their advice changes with the pressures upon them and the people chosen to lead them. They're always looking over their shoulders.'

The trout with the scar and his mate stopped quivering. They lay side by side as their high notes faded and the lights inside their heads became bleached and rinsed. Hamilton put her glass back on the table.

'If the natural environment were a commodity, its price would be rocketing because it is fast running out – but we don't even have a currency to value it in. We know the price of Mr Johnson's products. Someone knows what was paid for Sir John's land. Who could put a value on the view from Stinston Hill?'

Pearce turned again. 'Dame Vanessa Bennett, it was your letter to *The Times* that put this issue on the national agenda. You've got the last word.' The trout with the scar began to back away from his mate. The hen fish moved a little upstream and began to drive down on the gravel again in an attempt to make it lift and cover her eggs and hide them, but the stones did not move and the eggs lifted and bounced in the turbulence she made.

'Thank you. I'd like to make two points. Both follow from what Mrs Hamilton has said.

'The first is that nobody owns the earth. Every generation simply uses it and moves on – we're time-squatters, if you like. Recent generations, above all our own, have not used the earth well. We have created huge problems for those who come after us, long-term problems. The only people who could address problems like these – politicians and businessmen – are both driven by short-term pressures. We blame them, but in a sense it is dishonest to blame either.' The cameras cut away to show Sir John Plumpton and Earl Johnson nodding, then came back. 'The truth is we all want a softer life and shareholders want profit. We want them today – and if we don't get them, the politicians and the company directors are out on their necks. So they can't afford to get out of step with the rest of us. It's us who somehow have to change. The solutions we're looking for are not out there, they're inside you and me.'

The eggs that were being moved by the way the hen trout was thrashing on the gravels were bouncing and rolling into the silt around them. Lisa Pearce pressed a finger to her earpiece, listened to the voice coming from it and gestured at Dame Vanessa. 'I'm going to have to hurry you, I'm afraid. What was the other point you wanted to make?'

Dame Vanessa nodded back. 'My second point is that things don't have to be big in their own right to be important.' The egg that the hen trout caught with her tail wobbled up and caught the light before falling back to the silt.

'Actions like the creation of this development, however badly needed from an economic point of view, are almost certainly leading to losses we don't yet know about. We may well be producing small environmental changes which, although not significant in themselves, could one day become significant. All it would need would be for several minor events to compound one another or for something unexpected to change the context in which the smaller events take place. In either case we could suffer a loss we did not expect or start a chain of events we might not be able to control.' She acknowledged Pearce's signal to end. 'In short, I fear we're playing roulette with the life support systems that we all depend on. I fear that little by little we could be turning off the lights.'

Earl Johnson was speaking before Lisa Pearce could cut in. Dark clouds lifted around the hen fish as she worked. The cameras hesitated for a moment between Pearce and Johnson. She gave him a brief nod. 'Quickly, then.'

Johnson leaned forward and spoke in taut, crisp sentences that seemed to accentuate the urgency of the point he wanted to make. 'What Dame Vanessa is really saying is that she wants more caution, more balance, in our decision-making processes. At one level, I'm sure we'd all like that. But I suspect we're getting about as close to them as the real world will allow. The fact is we live in a jungle. We survive by competing and winning. It's sudden death out there. Others aren't going to stand around and watch while the UK hums and hahs about everything. I'm all for the environment. I'm concerned about global warming, the risks of genetic modification, pollution, abstraction and every-thing else. I've got kids of my own, for heaven's sake. But we can't risk slowing up if others are steaming ahead. That's the road to national ruin. Giving our children an economic future has to be part of our legacy to them, as well.'

Pearce looked straight into the camera, speaking directly to the viewer. 'I'm sorry. There we must end it. Another contentious subject and more strongly held views. But as ever in this series, no easy solutions. We would have no dilemma if there were. From all of us here in Farley, goodbye.'

The hen trout that had been covering her eggs with silt in her attempt to cover them with gravel, drifted downstream. She kept shaking her head from side to side and opening her jaws as though coughing or retching. Lisa Pearce was home and the studio lights were out before the dirt trapped in the fish's gills, worked free.

Year 5, February

The pheasant took the dog by surprise. She was moulded into the depression near the concrete bridge by the farm and had been dozing since dawn. She was so still and camouflaged that she could have been a mound of small stones casting shadows about themselves. Only the faint, horizontal line of her back suggested anything at all and the dog had not noticed that. Nor had the dog noticed the wrinkled eyelid flicker when he approached, nor had he seen it lift like a secret door in the pheasant's head so that the pheasant could watch him.

It was only when the dog saw the rabbit and let out a low, joyous whine and bounded almost on top of her that the pheasant lifted and whirred over the stream. And it was only then that the dog saw her and leapt and whirled and his teeth clashed on the absence behind her. It was only then that the dog knocked over the drum.

The young man at the farm would not be able to understand how the drum came to be on the bridge in the first place, never mind to have its top loose; but the drum fell sideways when the dog's leg caught it and the top rolled in a wide circle on the edge of its rim. The brown liquid from the drum raced over the bridge in a thin, loosened spillage and began to stream into the water. Even the smallest drops bloomed white as milk flowers when they hit the surface and their whiteness spread downstream like a mist.

It took no time for the mist to reach the last of the water crowfoot that survived upstream from Top Bend. The mist passed over the base of the plant and found only crawlers and sliders and soft-bodied things, but it took them. It swept through the middle of the plant and found only shrimps and a few caddis grubs and some soft-bodied things, but it took those also.

When the mist reached the tips of the plant which were the only parts of the plant still moving fast enough to stay free of silt, the white mist found Baetis nymphs jostling and nudging and climbing over one another for want of room and water caterpillars packed so densely that no part of the stems beneath them could be seen. The nymphs of the Baetis flies tried to dart away when the white mist came but were not quick enough and the mist burned a grey film over their eyes. The water caterpillars let go their hold and thrashed like cut worms.

All the way from the bridge where the empty drum was soon recovered and having its top screwed tightly

back on to the deeper water around Top Bend, the
nymphs of the grey-winged Baetis flies and the larvae
of the brown-winged caddis flies and the alder larvae
and the shrimps and every other vital thing let go and
were carried away. Only the water caterpillars stayed
behind, spinning like propellers on the ends of the
threads that had once held them safe beyond all
planned dangers.

Downstream, where the mist had lost its fire, the
trout that were spent from spawning and that were
lank and dark for want of food, tilted and lifted and slid
and turned, absorbing the food drifting inertly towards
them.

That evening, when the light had begun to ebb, the
trout that had fed well on the plenty so suddenly offered
in spite of its sharp taste, felt cramps beginning to seize
their guts and one by one obeyed the spasms that
wracked and bent them and drove them awkwardly
through the water.

Before daylight came again, all the great fish that had
fought for the special places in those parts of the stream
and the next biggest fish that had won the next-best
places and all the smaller fish and the older fish and the
fish that had already been sick anyway, drifted and
tumbled and turned stiffly on the water and were lost
in the emptiness of the drop over the falls.

Year 5, March

New buildings were racing up, even though as much rain had fallen through the winter as used to fall in winter. The maisonettes in Hanger Close were nearly finished. The last house in Frontage Fields had been occupied for weeks. The clubhouse for the new golf course already had its roof on and was vibrating like a drum skin to the scrapings and bangings going on inside.

Though the weather seemed back to normal and the Broadchalk and the Clearwater had risen because so many of the springs that fed them from the west and the east had also risen, the stream was still low.

The water in the ground that was so far away from the two rivers that it definitely had no links with either had already been drained lower than it was drained in the lifetime of the young man or the old man or his father or his father. It was drained lower than it had been in the lifetimes of the Fletchers or the Coopers or of anyone else who had farmed the land before them. It was drained lower than it had been in the lifetimes of Henry de Montfort and his feckless dog or in the lifetime of Claudius Nepos or in the lifetime of the man in the deer pelt who had given the perfectly round stone to the girl whose smile had been like the sun coming out. The water in the hills that gave rise to the springs that fed the stream was drained lower than it had been before the wolves had prowled there or the bears had roared there or the wild pigs had truffled in the loose-littered ground.

The springs that fed the stream were this low when the Baetis nymph clinging to the tip of the little water crowfoot plant near the fallen willow, let go because silt so fine that it could settle into every fold and dip and crevice of every stem had finally left nowhere for a nymph to move.

The hills were this empty and the springs were this low at the time the water caterpillar that lived not far from the place where the elk had eventually drowned in the swamp, died because the fine silts that were settling out from the slow water caught in her vital places and some other places and clogged them.

By the time work on the community centre was under way, the mayfly nymphs that had survived from the year before were constantly having to push and bundle away silt so fine that it wanted to float into their burrows and block them.

By the time the new shopping arcade was begun,

the stoneclinger that had constantly been edging side-ways from the east side of the old spawning gravels towards the middle had met the stoneclinger moving towards the middle from the west side. By the time the new health centre was being opened and the doctors were settling in, the two nymphs were side by side together on one of the few stones near the middle that were still free of silt. Even then they could get no food or peace because all the other stoneclingers that survived below the falls had edged out to the same small place and were jammed side-by-side together because there was nowhere else to go.

By the time the silt and chokeweed had laid a blanket over them all, the leech had arrived.

Year 5, April

The leech was still and outstretched. The green tinge in her flank blended perfectly into the chokeweed to her left and the brown tinge merged her perfectly into the side of the old tree stump that the flood had dropped.

She had spent a long time reaching that place and waited for a while as though resting. Then the leech unfurled the whole length of herself and stretched straight out from the side of the stump close to the fallen willow until she lay almost horizontal in the water. She held herself quite still save for the occasional slow, circling movements that her upper half made. The movements made her look as if she were scanning all around her, almost as if she were searching for something in particular.

At about the time Paul Tyler, the Whole-Site

Director, was greeting the Minister's public relations man, the leech registered the distant images that her four eyes were detecting.

Geoffrey Billings had insisted on coming to see everything for himself. He always did when the Minister was involved personally. The two men did not talk long. Tyler went through the history of the development, from the origins of the plans that had been dreamed up a generation before to the way the Government had wooed multinationals like Cogent Electronics, though it turned out Billings knew a lot more about that than he did. They talked through the protests and the legal hiccups and the latest on Lincoln and the problem at Durham that was soon to hit the fan. Tyler showed the graphs and tables that had charted progress over the years and talked of how lucky they had been with the weather. Billings asked about job numbers and community facilities and if there were any problems the Minister should be aware of, but Tyler said no.

It was as Billings was putting his papers back into his briefcase and was closing the lid with its upholstered click that the hen trout that had begun her journey from below the three posts and that had steadily moved upstream to find deep water, shrugged her way into the pool below the fallen willow.

All the fish in the pool saw the lank fish arrive, but they did not rise up and flare their gills because they were as weak as she was and some of them anyway had just arrived themselves. Even the trout with the scar that owned the pool and that had the place at the head of it had stopped whirling and flaring his gills when a new

219

fish came in because of the clutches in his empty gut and because of the great stone that filled his head.

And so all the trout in the pool below the fallen willow edged aside and moved a little upstream to make way when the hen fish from below the three posts arrived. The trout with the scar moved the necessary distance forward and a little to the side before Billings had even reached the door and said he had some time to kill and planned to drive up the valley to see things for himself.

It was about the time that the gaunt cock fish with the hooked jaw and the huge head moved close to the pool below the willow because he was seeking deeper water as well, that Tyler and Billings shook hands and parted.

It was as Tyler was ringing his wife to say he would be home early for once, just after Billings had passed the slip-road on the new motorway north of Stinston, that the gaunt cock fish with the hooked jaw and the huge head slid into the pool. It was when the gaunt cock fish with the hooked jaw arrived that all the other fish in the pool rearranged themselves again to make way and the images that had resolved into a known shape in each of the leech's four eyes came clearly into focus and the leech held herself tense and still.

While Geoffrey Billings was driving along the new motorway north of Stinston so that he could see everything for himself, though he was so far away from the stream that he could not see it at all, the trout with the scar edged a little nearer the lank weed and the old brown stump and the fish leech that had lain so perfectly camouflaged and still, clamped herself to him.

By the time Billings had returned to his office and

Tyler and his wife were enjoying their best talk in months over a drink before dinner, the leech that had attached herself to the trout with the scar was boring through the skin where the scale had come off and sensing the goodness of the juices beneath it.

Even as the leech was boring and drinking, the flukes were enjoying the wide, free waters of the right eye of the gaunt cock fish with the hooked jaw and the huge head and the fading sight, and the tapeworm in the gut of the hen fish from the three posts was appreciating the rich darkness of the home he had found and the larva of the spiny-headed worm was beginning to glow bright orange through the sides of the shrimp he was using as a host because that was what the law of continuing had required him to do.

It was all happening as finer silts than ever were settling out everywhere and as dead matter was gathering in the dark places and as the crawlers and the sliders and the soft-bodied things were multiplying beyond imagining and as the things that lived head-down in tubes with their back ends protruding were swaying as though dancing at the wonder of it all.

It all happened a little after the sun had returned hotter than ever and as the spring behind the farm began to falter.

Year 5, May

It was as though the plan had been completely ignored.

It was as though the water that had once flowed too quickly for chokeweed had been made to flow slowly for the chokeweed's sake. It was as though the water that had once been too cold to encourage chokeweed had deliberately been warmed. It was as though the water that had once had in it too few of the nutrients that chokeweed needed, had been deliberately given them in abundance. It was almost as if the stream had been deliberately ordered to sink into its bed so that what chemicals were in it should have less water to dilute them. Even the water that had once been too shaded for chokeweed had chokeweed in it because the trees had been felled and the sun now reached everywhere.

The chokeweed curved and wound in the water. The

bends and bays and dips in the bed might have been shaped in readiness for each strand and thread.

The chokeweed grew and the sun burned all through the time that the mayfly nymphs were trying to leave their burrows in the stream bed but could not. The only mayfly nymphs left anywhere lived alongside the island and opposite the shingle banks and downstream from the fallen willow and most of these were trapped in their tunnels by the tangled threads that grew over each entrance like a lain snare. Even the nymphs that managed to leave their tunnels died because they got caught in the threads and webs and the stabbers and the biters and the things that rejoiced were able to clamber up and reach them.

The sun burned hot as a brazier on the day that the old man moved to the village because of the young man's coming wedding, though it cast only a cool light through the blue glass roof above the new arcade where the old man sometimes sat on a bench and saw the convenience of the supermarket and the doctor's surgery and the chemist's shop and the leisure centre for the youngsters and all the other new facilities that had been built in no time.

The sun put rainbows in the spray that arched over the wide, flat fields from the pipes the young man had linked to boreholes of his own. It cast long, tilting shadows across the wall of the room where the family that only seemed to get together for weddings and funerals was talking after the young man and his bride and the other guests had gone.

The sun streamed in while they all talked about the wedding and the wonderful weather, then the old man said there was something unnatural about the heat and his bronzed young niece said it could stay unnatural for ever as far as she was concerned.

The sun slipped behind the small, white cloud while the old man's brother said everyone was saying it was to do with gases in the atmosphere or something and while his other brother was saying at least governments were getting together and talking about things now. The sun slid from behind the small cloud as the half-cousin from Australia who had to fly back the next day was saying that talking was all some governments ever would do and that there was masses of pollution to come yet because who believed China or India or anyone else would hold back their own growth while the West went on polluting to achieve growth of its own.

The sun dazzled the young woman in the corner so much that she had to shield her own eyes with one hand and the eyes of the little girl on her knee with the other. She said that if it really was something to do with changes in the climate because of gases in the atmosphere, the gases were already up there and could not be brought down and it was probably too late to change anything now. Nobody smiled when she said 'thank you one and all on behalf of my children' or when the spring behind the farm suddenly dropped.

Year 5, June

It was soon after the spring behind the farm dropped suddenly that the trout with the scar moved forward again; soon after the low water in the hills must have been drained below some critical point so that the stream seemed to sink softly into its bed and the brown line that wound down the whole of its length to the river widened noticeably and the top of the gnarled log where the salmon used to meet and lift and soar like young things, rose up through the surface like a dinosaur's back.

The trout with the scar moved so suddenly that the leeches seemed taken by surprise. The leech that was trying to get into his gills nearly lost her grip and the two holding themselves straight out from between his eyes like pointing antennae were swept back along his head in the slipstream he created.

When the trout with the scar and the huge head and the thin body and the leeches all over him moved forward, all the fish behind him moved forward as though attached to him by strings and towed.

There seemed a leadenness in them all. It was as though the hollowness in their long, thin flanks and the dullness in their eyes and the stones that every fish seemed to have in its head weighed them down; or that the water had somehow become thicker or more resistant when they moved their gills.

The gaunt trout that had been the first among the male fish to have a hooked jaw and a huge head and become blind in one eye followed the trout with the scar. The hen fish from below the three posts, the one that was beginning to look more like an eel, went after them.

Some other fish moved in behind the three big fish and then the little cock fish that was leaking fluids and odours he should not have had inside him followed, even though the threads of chokeweed kept reaching for him and stroking him. The little hen fish that carried the seeds of eggs that could never mature moved forward behind the little cock fish, even though the chokeweed here and there draped itself over her eyes and fingered her gills and tried to get into her mouth when she opened it. The tiniest of the fish in the stream followed, keeping low.

It was, when they moved, as though the stream had been reduced to grottos and caves. It was as though the world had been draped with green rags and brown rags and was closing in; as though everywhere the fish went, tentacles explored them and sly fingers caressed.

All the fish that had gathered in the pool by the willow moved towards the falls on the day that the main landscaping began in readiness for the Minister's visit. It was the thing in the water that made them go: the thing in the water and the pressure on their gills and the clutches that kept catching at their hearts at night. It was the images that the law of continuing had put inside them when they were young that drew them on. The big fish saw in their heads again the boiling whiteness of the falls and the coolness of the water and the lightness that the fizzing bubbles made. The younger fish followed because the big fish went.

When all the fish had passed around the end of the stump where the leech had lain in ambush; when they had passed through the shaft of sunlight that slanted through the space in the webbed roof and they had all seen the mites and the fleas and the small creatures that pedalled through it wondrously lit; when they had forced their way through the places on the stream bed where the water raced as though through tunnels because the chokeweed hemmed it in and pressed it down; when they had edged around the stiff fish that was jammed sideways in front of them with its wide eyes grey and with its jaws gagged open and with the threads of chokeweed caught on its teeth; when they had eventually entered the dim grotto beneath the place where the martins used to nest and had settled again among the webs and the torn rags and the tentacles that explored and the fingers that caressed, the little cock fish that was partly a hen fish, wobbled.

It was not a great movement. It was simply that the little fish that had for a long time seemed to be finding the thickness of the water too much and the pressure on his gills too great, moved a little forward and wobbled a little and righted himself.

All the fish in the long line ahead of him caught the flash from the little trout's flank and some tilted around the dishes of their eyes to see what it was, but most looked straight ahead as though their eyes were leaden.

The little trout lay still for a long time after that, pressing out with his gills as hard as he could against the thing in the water that seemed to press them in. Then, as evening approached and the gloom about him deepened, the little cock fish that had been changed in his secret places in a way no fish should have been changed and that had been putting confusing odours into the water since he had been born, wobbled again and became agitated.

The little cock fish moved as though seized and used. He dashed forward and whirled around and around and looped and spiralled near the trout with the scar, though neither the trout with the scar nor any of the fish behind him turned to look.

When the little fish had swum in wide circles with his mouth wide open and had righted himself again and then turned on his side and swum downstream twitching, the strange odours his body squeezed from him became stronger than ever but no fish, not even the male fish, took any notice.

When the sun had gone and the law of continuing had reminded the chokeweed of the plan; when the chokeweed had stopped changing carbon dioxide into oxygen as it had all day and instead began to pour out carbon dioxide as required of it at night; when the thickness in the water thickened and the thing in the water began to press on their gills so hard that their hearts pounded and faltered and clutched with the stress of breathing; when the stones that hung about the other fish held the other fish so fast to the stream bed that they could not have made themselves move even if they had wanted to move, the little cock fish and one of the medium-sized fish from the middle of the queue that had also begun to wobble, both wobbled again.

The little cock fish that had been changed inside by the stains in the water that he could not see or smell and the medium-sized fish from the middle of the queue that had two grey eyes because of all the flukes in them, began to swim and stop and swim side-by-side together, though neither fish was going anywhere that it had decided to go and the medium-sized fish could not have seen anyway because she was blind.

The little cock fish that had been changed in places where no changes should have been made and the medium-sized fish that was blind raced around in tight circles and wobbled and darted. Then the little cock fish began to spiral and loop through the water that was too thick to breathe in and the blind fish turned on her back and swam upside down with her mouth open as though the thing in the water was keeping it open.

Before the night was over and David Hoffmeyer had even left his hotel, the medium-sized fish lay broadside on the bottom without moving and the little cock fish lay high in the water and was sucking at the surface as though drinking in air.

cock fish, nor to notice the bubbles that welled behind its gills and that kept catching the light and bending it into colours. The trout with the scar that lay leaden and weak and closed in on himself did not see the little cock fish stop moving soon after the sun had lit the trees on the skyline again and David Hoffmeyer had reached the airport.

Neither the trout with the scar nor any of the other fish, not even the bullheads nor the loaches nor the minnows that were always on the lookout because they were always in danger, saw Hoffmeyer's helicopter clattering overhead or knew when it dropped onto the pad in the Broadchalk valley.

None of the fish was aware when Hoffmeyer announced that the site would be extended again because the new products were such a success and none of them heard Earl Johnson telling him that the water problem they thought might be a problem would be no problem at all.

Not a single fish heard the helicopter clattering back overhead but lower, or saw the heat of its exhaust or smelled it, or felt the hot breath that swept through the high corn like a rumour.

Year 5, July

It was as Peter Althorpe was telling the Lincoln inquiry that attitudes had to change or else there would soon be no green fields left and not an ancient brick upon an ancient brick, that all the fish that remained in the stream gathered at last in the pool beneath the falls.

It was as Althorpe was sitting down and Simon Goode was standing up that the water in the pool dropped suddenly, exactly as if the springs in the high hills had passed another critical point.

On the day the last of the wide, flat fields to be ready for harvesting again was being harvested and the fields on either side of that were being ploughed again, the great spring behind the farm suddenly dropped to a trickle.

It was after the shower had started and the hedge

around the farm was being slung with cut light, that the next spring stopped.

The water that had once tumbled and roared and fizzed with white bubbles, curved over the falls like bent glass thinly and the fish that had come in search of it seemed seized with a panic. They jostled head-down to get where the last bubbles bloomed and their tails thrashed the surface just behind them.

Year 5, August

The chokeweed began to die soon after the weather changed, just as the law of continuing had required in the plan.

On the night that the flowers were being planted out by floodlight and the displays were being put up in those buildings that Tyler and Billings had agreed the Minister should visit, the fish were finding it so hard to move their gills that the water might have been turned to syrup.

The law of continuing had not told the fish how extra oxygen was consumed when chokeweed decayed and that a shortage of oxygen could easily result. It had not mentioned that an oxygen shortage was always made much worse at night when plants were putting out less oxygen anyway. It had not even mentioned how the

233

effects of these two could be made worse beyond imagining if they happened at a time when the water was
warm and had less oxygen in it to start with. But still,
every fish had been told all that it needed to know about
the importance of keeping its gills moving and the thing
in the water that was already rampant reminded them
one by one.

Though the law of continuing had told the trout with
the scar and all the other fish as much as they needed
to know, the trout with the scar seemed too preoccupied
with himself to take notice of anything.

The trout with the scar did not see the gaunt trout
with the hooked jaw and the huge head and the one
blind eye suddenly drive his nose into the stream bed
and stir up the dark clouds, or even feel the fish's tail
thrumming against his flank before it stopped.

The trout with the scar did not sense the little hen
fish that carried the eggs that could never have matured,
drifting away upside down before she began to spiral
and loop.

The trout with the scar did not know that the hen fish
from behind the three posts had rolled onto her side and
had been driven forward and had spiralled so far into
the chokeweed that she became only a pulse of green
light.

The lank trout with the scar that had the leeches all
over him and the tapeworms in his belly and the stone
in his head and one good eye because parasites had
commandeered the other, saw nothing of the way all the
fish in the pool were beginning to pitch and tumble. He
did not see the leeches and the worms and the soft-
bodied things and the things that stood up in tubes

swaying as though dancing at the wonder of it all. He heard nothing of the gulls that dived and screamed and backed away from one another, tugging.

The trout with the scar knew nothing because of the way each breath had become a shallower breath since that night had begun. He had already been taken by the thing that was everywhere in the water and that had locked him in his own tight curve and sent him looping stiffly into the margins.

By the time the announcement was being made about the new medical research centre to be built at Farley from money not spent on a tunnel at Stinston, the trout with the scar had no conscious movement left in him.

By the time Nick Brewster of Cogent Electronics was staring into the bottom of his glass in Kuala Lumpur because his wife had just called him to say she wanted a better life and a divorce, the trout with the scar was being seized again and again by the thing in the water that the heat and the pumps and all else had created.

As Paul Tyler and Geoffrey Billings were making their respective final checks and the Minister was looking for the first time at the notes prepared for him and Dame Vanessa Bennett was telling the *Guardian* that the only hope in the long term was for human beings to change their behaviour but that to ask them to change their behaviour was tantamount to asking them to change their nature, the trout with the scar was being driven head-first into the chokeweed because his tail had acquired a will of its own.

By the time the Minister and David Hoffmeyer were smalltalking about the importance of governments and industry working together and Simon Goode the biologist was writing his paper on butterflies, the trout with the scar that was lying on his side with silt in his throat was rising up on the chokeweed because the weed was compressing beneath him.

By the time the Minister was putting on his hard hat because the pictures of him cutting the ribbon would look better if he did and the man in Gothenburg who was so fascinated by England was frying an egg, the chokeweed had made a pillow for the trout with the scar and the spasms of his gills and the jerkings of his tail had eased him onto it.

As Lisa Pearce was framing the shot that would show the scissors on the ribbon in close-up with the crowd behind and Jo Hamilton was going shopping because she could see nothing to celebrate and the Curator of Farley museum was seeing how well the artefacts found at the Frontage looked in their specially designed cases and the trout with the scar was gasping, the water in the stream that the law of continuing had created, shrank further. It left the dome of the great fish's eye exposed above the surface and the sun began to dry it.

As the Minister took the scissors and stepped towards the ribbon, the trout with the scar in the stream that had been planned before the wolves had prowled there or the bears had roared there or the wild pigs had truffled in the loose-littered ground, stopped splashing.

As the Minister opened the scissors with his right hand and offered the ribbon to them with his left and paused and smiled this way and that for the cameras, the tail of the trout in the stream that had flowed as clear as melted time through meadowsweet and hemp agrimony, through burr reed and brooklime, through purple loosestrife and flag iris and cress, trembled and fretted and arranged itself slowly.

The eye of the trout that the kingfisher had scarred tilted forward. The crowd pressed closer, anxious to miss nothing.

As the cut ribbon separated and the silken ends fluttered, the eye of the trout that had lived as quick and light as water itself, stared sightlessly as though at something finally arrived, then rolled loosely back.

The dome of the sky looked down at it.

And the applause rang out.

THE END